WILLIAM

SHAKESPEARE'S

THE **PHANTOM** OF **MENACE**

STAR WARS*

PART THE FIRST

WILLIAM SHAKESPEARE'S

THE **PHANTOM** OF **MENACE**

STAR WARS
PART THE FIRST

By Ian Doescher

INSPIRED BY THE WORK OF GEORGE LUCAS
AND WILLIAM SHAKESPEARE

QUIRK BOOKS
PHILADELPHIA

Copyright © 2015 by Lucasfilm Ltd. & TM. All rights reserved.
Used under authorization.

Library of Congress Cataloging in Publication Number: 2014953126

ISBN: 978-1-59474-806-6

Printed in the United States of America

Typeset in Sabon

Text by Ian Doescher
Illustrations by Nicolas Delort
Production management by John J. McGurk

Quirk Books
215 Church Street
Philadelphia, PA 19106
quirkbooks.com

10 9 8 7 6 5 4 3

TO ETHAN YOUNGERMAN, BARD OF NEW YORK,

AND TO CHRIS MARTIN, JEDI OF THE SOUTH.

TO HEIDI ALTMAN, FORCE IN OLD D.C.,

AND TO NAOMI WALCOTT, FAR-FLUNG MUSE

DRAMATIS PERSONAE

CHORUS
RUMOR

YODA, *a Jedi Master*
QUI-GON JINN, *a Jedi Knight*
OBI-WAN KENOBI, *his Jedi apprentice*
MACE WINDU *and* KI-ADI-MUNDI, *Jedi Knights*
QUEEN PADMÉ AMIDALA, *of Naboo*
SABÉ, *her handmaiden and decoy*
ANAKIN SKYWALKER, *a boy of Tatooine*
SHMI SKYWALKER, *his mother*
R2-D2, *a droid*
C-3PO, *a droid*
KITSTER, SEEK, AMEE, *and* WALD, *friends of Anakin*
SIO BIBBLE, *governor of Naboo*
CAPTAIN PANAKA *and* RIC OLIÉ, *gentlemen of Naboo*
BOSS NASS, *ruler of the Gungan tribe*
JAR JAR BINKS, *a Gungan clown*
CAPTAIN TARPALS, *a Gungan soldier*
CHANCELLOR VALORUM, *of the Senate*
SENATOR PALPATINE/DARTH SIDIOUS, *a senator of Naboo and Sith Lord*
DARTH MAUL, *a Sith*
NUTE GUNRAY, *viceroy of the Trade Federation*
DAULTAY DOFINE, RUNE HAAKO, *and* TEY HOW,
   gentlemen of the Trade Federation
WATTO, *a tradesman of Tatooine*
SEBULBA, *a sportsman of Tatooine*
JABBA OF THE HUTT, *a gangster*
FODE AND BEED, *commentators*

PODRACERS, SENATORS, PILOTS, GUARDS, THE QUEEN'S
HANDMAIDENS, GUNGANS, DROIDS, *and* CREATURES

PROLOGUE.

Outer space.

Enter CHORUS.

CHORUS   Alack! What dreadful turmoil hath beset
The strong Republic and its bonds of peace.
O'er distant trade routes all do sigh and fret
As fears of grim taxation do increase.
The greedy, vile Trade Federation hath   5
Created a blockade none may pass through.
With deadly battleships they block the path
Unto the little planet call'd Naboo.
Whilst politicians endlessly debate,
The Chancellor Supreme plies strategy.   10
He sends two Jedi to negotiate—
They who keep peace within the galaxy.
In time so long ago begins our play,
In troubl'd galaxy far, far away.
                                  [Exit.

SCENE 1.

Aboard the Republic cruiser and aboard the
Trade Federation battleship.

Enter RUMOR.

RUMOR   Open your hearts; for which of you will stop
The vent of feeling when loud Rumor speaks?
Her flaming tongue with poison'd tip shall drop
Unrest from Tatooine to Naboo's peaks.
See how, with mere suggestion of a tax,   5
Begin star wars that shall your eyes amaze.
Enraging th'Federation with false facts
Good sport did make for Rumor's cunning ways—
Inciting the Republic to respond
Now sets the game afoot on ev'ry side.   10
Thus shall I cause new worries to be spawn'd:
Hint of a dark Force rising I'll provide,
E'en till the proud Republic longeth for
Protection from some unknown, looming threat.
Replete with fear, each heart shall be full sore   15
Ere I have ceas'd the worry I beget.
Quick now, and let this merry play begin—
Unveil the Empire's full prehistory!
E'en groundlings, waiting weeks to be let in,
Look forward to the wonders they shall see.   20
Starts now what you have long'd for, sans delay:
Attend—a phantom menace comes anon!
Ye shall be pull'd into our clever play,
Ears, hearken to this story that doth dawn.

                                                  [Exit.

Enter QUI-GON JINN, OBI-WAN KENOBI, PILOT, *and* CAPTAIN.

QUI-GON	I say, good captain.
CAPTAIN	—Aye, sir, what's your will? 25
QUI-GON	Pray, make communication unto this
	Trade Federation battleship, e'en here.
	Tell them that we would board their ship anon.

       [The captain addresses Nute Gunray via comlink.

CAPTAIN	With great respect and humble mien, good sir,
	With awe for the Trade Federation's might, 30
	The brave ambassadors would swiftly board
	Your ship, with your permission and consent.
QUI-GON	[*aside:*] Methinks this captain's words are oversweet.
NUTE	[*through comlink:*] Indeed—we nothing herein have

                                to hide,

	And as you know full well, our blockade is 35
	Within the bounds of the Republic's law.
	Your kind ambassadors shall be receiv'd
	As we would welcome all Republic guests.

           [Exit Nute Gunray from comlink.

QUI-GON	Thus shall we fly unto their battleship
	And land within the core of its vast frame. 40
	These Federation ships are massive, aye,
	And run to excess for a mere blockade.
	Yet, when taxation is the greater theme,
	The melody oft leans toward life or death.
	It is an ancient song that all know well— 45
	The notes of levies ring with morbid knoll.
	Indeed, it may most verily be said
	That only death and taxes certain are.

      [The Republic ship lands inside the battleship.
          Many droids surround the ship.

Enter DROID TC-14 *to speak with* QUI-GON JINN *and* OBI-WAN
KENOBI. PILOT *and* CAPTAIN *remain in the Republic ship.*

TC-14   My name is TC-14, at your aid.
                 I prithee, come with me, good gentlemen.   50
                 Your visit doth bring honor unto us,
                 Ambassadors of high and noble blood.
                 Be now at ease, and wait upon my lord,
                 For he shall hither come to speak with you.
                                              [Exit TC-14.

OBI-WAN   I have a feeling bad about this, Master.   55
QUI-GON   Yet sense I nothing. Wherefore art thou tense?
OBI-WAN   'Tis not about the mission—something else.
                 Elusive 'tis, aye, difficult to name.
QUI-GON   O, center not on thy anxiety,
                 Young Obi-Wan. Thy concentration here   60
                 Maintain—within this very moment now—
                 For such is where thy focus doth belong.
OBI-WAN   But Master Yoda hath instructed me
                 To be e'er mindful of the future, for
                 Its advent may have meaning in my life.   65
QUI-GON   'Tis true, yet future possibility
                 Must not be kept within the forefront of
                 Thy mind at the expense of what is here:
                 The present moment. Be e'er mindful of
                 The living Force, my worthy Padawan.   70
OBI-WAN   Aye, Master. Then, unto the present time:
                 How do you think the Viceroy shall respond
                 Unto the noble Chancellor's demands?
QUI-GON   Methinks there can be little doubt in this:
                 These Federation dogs are cowardly   75

And shall be quick to heel at our command.
Negotiation shall be swift, indeed.

Enter NUTE GUNRAY, DAULTAY DOFINE, *and* TC-14 *above on balcony.*

NUTE   What didst thou say, thou terror-speaking droid?
TC-14   Just what my sockets hath observ'd, my lord:
            These two ambassadors are Jedi Knights.   80
DAULTAY   This I did prophesy in my mind's eye:
            The two have come to force a settlement.
NUTE   Go thou and make some keen distraction there;
            I must make contact with Lord Sidious.
DAULTAY   Hast thou lost all thy pow'r of intellect,   85
            Thou jarring fool-born simple-minded rogue?
            I shall not go where Jedi's steps do tread.
            Instead, send one insensible to fear:
            This droid shall serve our purpose. [*To TC-14:*] Go,
                                                    anon!
                                    [*Exit TC-14 from balcony.*

OBI-WAN   Is it their nature, so to make us wait?   90
QUI-GON   Nay, truly I do sense a fear too grand
             For such a wee affair as trade disputes.

                    Enter TC-14, with serving tray.

TC-14   [*aside:*] I serve the drinks these Jedi to appease
             And in so doing serve my masters' will.
             We droids are here to serve: 'tis protocol,   95
             Yet here my service lacketh etiquette,
             For it doth serve these Jedi to deceive.
                    [*TC-14 serves drinks to Qui-Gon and Obi-Wan.*

        Enter DARTH SIDIOUS *in beam on balcony, speaking with*
                  NUTE GUNRAY *and* DAULTAY DOFINE.

SIDIOUS   What is't?
DAULTAY   —The scheme that you have schem'd hath fail'd,
             Lord Sidious. Our ruse—e'en this blockade—
             Is finish'd, for would we dare fight against   100
             The Jedi? Nay! It would be foolishness.
SIDIOUS   [*to Nute Gunray:*] Hear me now, Viceroy: I'll not
                                           have this filth,
             This stunted slime of rank and worthless nerve,
             This craven, simple-minded lump of flesh
             Within my presence e'er again. Put not   105
             Such weak examples of resolve and will
             Before a mighty Sith.
                                   [*Exit Daultay Dofine.*
                         This recent twist
             Of Fate's blind spinning wheel hath luckless been.

We must, therefore, accelerate our plans:
Begin to send the troops unto Naboo.   110

NUTE   My lord, your words astound! For shall the law
              Be with us in this action we shall take?

SIDIOUS   I tell thee, I am arbiter and law:
              It shall be legal if I make it so.

NUTE   What shall be done with these two Jedi, then?   115

SIDIOUS   'Twas ill-conceivèd of the chancellor
              To bring the Jedi into this affair.
              Hear my command and follow: kill them both!

NUTE   Indeed, my lord: as you wish, it shall be.

                    [Exit Darth Sidious from beam.
                              Exit Nute Gunray.

          Enter PILOT and CAPTAIN, aside in Republic ship.

PILOT   Alas, good captain, look upon the guns—   120
              They turn in our direction. We are slain!

CAPTAIN   Raise shields, my man, to grant us some defense.

PILOT   Too late, too late!
                    [The Trade Federation guns fire on the
                  Republic ship, killing Pilot and Captain. Qui-Gon
                        and Obi-Wan brandish their lightsabers.

QUI-GON   —What villainy is this?
              My senses tell of some abrupt attack.

OBI-WAN   I sense it, too, my master. I believe   125
              Our comrades have been kill'd whilst they did wait.
                    [Gas begins to seep into the room.

QUI-GON   And what is more, now comes a vapor rank!
              Dioxin—poison'd gas. Pray, hold thy breath!
                    [The Jedi hold their breath.

Enter BATTLE DROIDS *including* OWO-1, *standing at attention outside door. Enter* NUTE GUNRAY *in beam.*

NUTE   [*to battle droids:*] For certain they are dead by now—
                                                              since these
                    Two Jedi are not politicians, they   130
                    Are not with hot air fill'd, and thus have not
                    The stores of breath essential to survive.
                    Still: go, destroy what remnant may remain.
                            [*Exit Nute Gunray from beam. The door opens.*
                                TC-14 passes through the doorway
                                        and sees the battle droids.
TC-14   I beg your pardon, droids of mettle made.
OWO-1   Go forth, investigate, good corporal.   135
DROID 1   Forsooth, forsooth!
                            [*The Jedi come forth suddenly, fighting.*

Enter NUTE GUNRAY, RUNE HAAKO, *and* TEY HOW *aside on bridge.*

OWO-1   —Fight for our masters true!
NUTE   What now—the monitors have been destroy'd?
                    What circumstance unhappy doth befall?
TEY   Transmission hath been wholly lost, my liege!
RUNE   [*to Nute:*] Hast thou e'er had a clash with Jedi
                                                              Knights?   140
NUTE   Nay, truly not till now. Thy warning doth
                    Give me some pause. [*To Tey:*] Seal off the bridge
                                                              entire!
TEY   Indeed!
RUNE   —Dost thou not see? 'Tis not enough.
NUTE   And call a host of droidekas anon!

RUNE   Yet thou art deaf, and in thy panic shalt   145
            Not listen to the truth: we'll not survive.
                        [*The bridge doors are sealed as the Jedi*
                                continue to fight and advance.

OBI-WAN   The battle droids are worthless when fac'd by
            The power of the Force. All are o'erthrown!

QUI-GON   Indeed, now may my lightsaber be to
            This door the key, that we may entrance make.   150
                        [*Qui-Gon uses his lightsaber to*
                                bore through the bridge door.

NUTE   Behold, they come! Swift, close the blast doors. Aye,
            For certain that shall keep the two at bay
            Until the fearsome droidekas appear.

QUI-GON   The lightsaber cuts not as't did before—
            Belike another door hath seal'd the way.   155
            Well play'd, shrewd sirs, and yet not well enough:
            Observe the power of a burning sun,
            This mystic beam I wield here in my hand.
                        [*Qui-Gon pushes his lightsaber directly*
                                through the center of the door.

NUTE   They still make headway—how is't possible?

RUNE   Where are the droidekas thou summon'd forth?   160

            Enter DROIDEKAS.

OBI-WAN   My master, look—destroyer droids approach!
                        [*Qui-Gon pulls his lightsaber from the door to face*
                                the droidekas, which begin shooting at the Jedi.
            They generate their own strong shields, too. Fie!

QUI-GON   We parry ev'ry blast; they'll not break through.
            But neither are we close enough to strike

And their strong shields do block what we reflect.   165
'Tis but an errant game that none can win.
So let us fly and find another way.
                              [Exeunt Qui-Gon and Obi-Wan.

RUNE   The droidekas have sent them fleeing, ha!
TEY   Sir, I report: the Jedi speedily
Retreat unto the ventilation shaft.   170
                              [Exeunt Nute Gunray,
                              Rune Haako, and Tey How.

Enter QUI-GON JINN *and* OBI-WAN KENOBI *to the*
main hangar above, on balcony.

QUI-GON   Do you behold this here, young Obi-Wan?
'Tis battle droids—and hundreds, mayhap more.
OBI-WAN   Indeed, an army for invasion made.
QUI-GON   This is a strategy most strange for the
Trade Federation. By my troth, this strange   175
And unexpected twist doth warrant care.
We must inform the innocent Naboo
And Chancellor Valorum, too. Hear this,
My young apprentice: let us split our paths
And use these ships as transport to Naboo   180
Where, on the planet's surface, we shall meet.
OBI-WAN   Aye, Master, I shall do as you command,
And rendezvous with you upon Naboo.
What's more—your foresight wise they could not
                                             thwart:
Negotiations were, indeed, quite short.   185
                              [Exeunt.

SCENE 2.

On the planet Naboo and aboard the Trade Federation battleship.

Enter QUEEN AMIDALA.

AMIDALA   A person young is thought to have no pow'r,
             E'en when she is a queen, as like myself.
             Those older do surround, e'er pressing in
             And questioning each word that I do speak.
             One thinks I shall a poor decision make,   5
             Another thinks himself more competent.
             The best of them do bow and show respect
             And treat me with the def'rence due my throne,
             Yet even their eyes speak of disbelief—
             Their courtesy becomes a stifling thing.   10
             A youth is no more frail than older folk,
             No less intelligent, no less sublime.
             Our steps are newer, yet we are no jewel
             To be protected and encas'd by them.
             We know of violence and life's harsh ways,   15
             Our tears descend in grief as their tears do.
             We are not made of softer stuff than they,
             The moods we feel oft run irate and rough.
             We have no thoughts less noble than our elders'—
             In truth, compassion may we ably teach.   20
             Then why is't thought that youth are so beneath
             Those older than we are, of any rank?
             'Tis foolishness, yea, 'tis foul treachery!
             If e'er these older ones could look within
             And plumb the depths of youth, what wonders would 25
             Before their eyes appear: the courage, strength

And valor it requires to be a youth:
The daily struggle to survive amid
The thousand constant doubts we do receive
From ev'ry person, e'en those who are dear,   30
The ever-present skirmishes with those
Of our own age, who should support and praise
Us, bound within the sacred bond of youth,
But who, instead, do injure with harsh words.
To be a youth within a world run by   35
An older generation taketh strength—
Yea, that beyond a hundred elders' might.
To be both youth and leader truly is
To be a target ever in their sights.
I would not trade my station for the world,   40
Nor would I wish it on mine enemy.
Although the path is fraught, this is our cause:
We youth shall mold the future we desire.
                    [*Queen Amidala presses a comlink switch.*

Enter NUTE GUNRAY, RUNE HAAKO, *and* TEY HOW,
above on balcony in Trade Federation battleship.

TEY   Transmission from the planet of Naboo.
RUNE   It is Queen Amidala—aye, herself.   45
NUTE   At last, we shall begin to see results,
           For speaking to the head shall move the body.
           [*To Amidala:*] Again, you come before us,
                                        highness grand.
AMIDALA   I do. Yet thou shalt not be pleas'd when thou
           Hast heard what I intend to say to thee.   50
           Thine errant boycott of our planet's through.

NUTE	Your words are naught but deep surprise to me,
	For of our failure I've heard no report.
AMIDALA	I am aware that the ambassadors
	Who were by Chancellor Valorum sent 55
	Have come to thee, and thou art order'd to
	Come to a settlement o'er this blockade.
NUTE	And yet, I know of no ambassadors.
	For certain, you have made a gross mistake.
AMIDALA	[*aside:*] Alas, have all our plans been thwarted then? 60
	[*To Nute Gunray:*] Beware, I warn thee, Viceroy,
	for 'tis true:
	The Federation hath made steps too bold.
NUTE	I know not what you mean, good lady queen:
	We would do nothing sans the Senate's say.
	As doth befit your youth and woman's fear 65
	Your Highness doth assume too much, indeed.
AMIDALA	O, we shall see how mine assumptions fare.
	[Exit Queen Amidala.
RUNE	In troth, the lady is correct. The Senate—
NUTE	'Tis far too late! What's done can't be undone.
RUNE	Aye, so! But do you think she doth expect
	The swift attack that we are bound to make? 70
NUTE	Nay, I know not. Yet this, at least, is clear:
	We must disrupt communication to
	The planet, lest they learn of our intent.
	[Exeunt Nute Gunray, Rune Haako, and Tey How.

Enter QUEEN AMIDALA *with* SIO BIBBLE, CAPTAIN PANAKA, COURT, *and* ATTENDANTS. *Enter* SENATOR PALPATINE *in beam.*

PALPATINE	What is't you say? Negotiations have
	Not reach'd a starting point because the two 75

Ambassadors did ne'er arrive? But nay,
How could that tale be true? The chancellor
Himself inform'd me that th'ambassadors
Most surely did arrive. Negotiate—

                           [Exit Palpatine from beam.

AMIDALA   I prithee, Senator, where hast thou gone?   80
              [*To Captain Panaka:*] What is the matter? What hath
                                    happen'd here?

PANAKA   [*to attendant:*] Check our transmission generator, lad.
SIO   If our communication hath been breach'd
              It means but one thing only: an attack.

AMIDALA   The Federation would not go so far,   85
              For such a move would mean their suicide.

PANAKA   I do agree: the Senate would revoke
              The Federation's trade ability,
              Which would destroy their commerce all at once.

AMIDALA   Negotiation must be our fond hope.   90
SIO   Negotiation, Highness? We have lost
              Communication, and as yet we know
              Of no ambassadors who have brought suit
              Unto the Federation for our sake.

AMIDALA   [*aside:*] O how he sneers and mocks mine utterance   95
           As he would never do were I his age.

PANAKA   The situation is most grave, my queen.
           If an invasion comes, the meager, slight
           Security our volunteers provide
           Shall be no contest for the harden'd ranks   100
           The Federation surely shall employ.

AMIDALA   I hear thee, counselors, and may hear more,
           But will condone no move that leads to war.

                                         [*Exeunt.*

SCENE 3.

On the planet Naboo.

Enter BATTLE DROIDS, *including* OOM-9.
Enter NUTE GUNRAY *and* RUNE HAAKO *in beam.*

OOM-9   How may I serve you, Viceroy? What's your will?

RUNE   Pay heed now, Captain. We have search'd the ship
           And found no trace of Jedi Knights therein.
           'Tis possible they hide aboard thy craft.

OOM-9   If they are here, good sir, we shall detect   5
           Them and destroy them as we were enjoin'd.

NUTE   Pray, use thou caution—underestimate
           These Jedi at thy peril. Vigilance!

           [*Exeunt Nute Gunray and Rune Haako from beam.*

Enter QUI-GON JINN, *hidden.*

QUI-GON   With hundreds of these battle droids I fly

Unto the planet that doth wait below.   10
Yea, unbeknownst to its kind citizens
Attack doth cruelly come to break their peace.
The craft hath landed. Run, e'er we are found!
      [Qui-Gon begins to run from the craft amid
      fleeing falumpasets, pursued by battle droids.

    Enter JAR JAR BINKS, *hidden, seeing* QUI-GON JINN.

JAR JAR   A man approacheth, cloth'd in Jedi garb.
      Belike this man brings aid unto Naboo   15
      Such as will help my people and my land.
      Mayhap this is the chance I have desir'd!
      For I have wander'd lo these many months
      A'thinking o'er this planet's dreary fate:
      Two peoples separated by their fear   20
      And prejudice, which e'er doth make us shirk
      From giving help unto each other. Aye,
      It may be that the only hope for us
      To be united is to realize
      That our two fates are tightly knit as one.   25
      Perchance this Jedi, follow'd by these droids,
      Doth bring the words to break our deep mistrust.
      I shall make introduction, in my way—
      Portray the part that I have learn'd so well:
      It doth befit the human prejudice   30
      To think we Gungans simple, low, and rude.
      I shall approach him thusly, yet shall bend
      Him to the path that shall assist us all.
      Put on thy simple wits now, Jar Jar Binks:
      Thus play the role of clown to stoke his pride.   35

[Jar Jar stands in Qui-Gon's path. Qui-Gon runs
into him and the two fall as the battle-droids
transport passes by over them.

          [*To Qui-Gon:*] O moiee-moiee, I so luvee!

QUI-GON   Thou brainless knave! Almost thou kill'd us both.

JAR JAR   I speakee, speakee, look at mee-mee!

QUI-GON   That thou canst speak doth not yet make thee wise.

          Now, go ye hence. Away!   40

JAR JAR   [*aside:*]   —Your kind did teach

          Me human language, and my profit on't

          Is I know how to move your human heart.

          So shall I speak most like a Gungan plain

          And thus disarm you by a fool's deceit.   45

          [*To Qui-Gon:*] Nay, nay, wise sir, O meesa stayee!

          O meesa callee Jar Jar Binks—see

          Now meesa is your servant humble.

QUI-GON   'Tis quite unnecessary, simple beast.

JAR JAR   O nay, it izzee necessary.   50

          Commanded by da gods it izzee.

     Enter OBI-WAN KENOBI, *pursued by two* BATTLE DROIDS.
          QUI-GON JINN *destroys the droids.*

          Now twicee you a'save my lifee.

OBI-WAN   [*to Qui-Gon:*] What creature, friend, is this?

QUI-GON   —A local, aye,

          A piteous native with a simple mind.

          Now let us hence afore more droids arrive.   55

JAR JAR   Did ee say more an more? Exquize me . . .

          [*Aside:*] And now to cast the line that plants the hook.

          [*To the Jedi:*] The safes' place is Gunga citee.

          'Tis where I grew, a hidden citee.

QUI-GON	Mayhap this lackwit may have purpose yet. 60
	A city? Canst thou take us there, kind brute?
JAR JAR	Ahh nay, as I me thinkee . . . nay, nay.
QUI-GON	And wherefore not, amphibious buffoon?
JAR JAR	O 'tis embarrassee, me banish'd.
	If I return and see de bosses 65
	Den dey will work me woe. You gettee?

                              [A sound is heard in the distance.

QUI-GON	Dost thou hear that grave sound? It is the noise
	Made by a thousand thousand woes to come.
OBI-WAN	If they discover us, we shall be crush'd
	And ground into a million fleshy bits. 70
	Oblivion shall be our final home.
JAR JAR	Ye makee good the pointee. Dis way!

             [The Jedi walk in the direction Jar Jar points.

[*Aside:*] These men have prejudice deep in their hearts,
For looking on me, they see savagery.
A "native," "local," "piteous," "buffoon";   75
With such dark slurs they slander my whole race.
Yet, Gungans quickly shall destroyèd be
If this attack doth touch our soggy home;
Belike the Jedi are our only hope.
Thus—though I was cast out for mine ideas   80
And have for many moons gone wandering
Above the waters of my home, where I
Have studied human ways and learn'd their speech—
I shall return to make amends and bring
These Jedi to the people to whom I   85
Am bound. So may I save my race entire.
To thine own kind be true, so say I e'er.
Give ev'ry man thine ear, but few thy voice—

At least the voice that speaketh with wise words.
Let them hear only speech of ruffian.   90
My truer voice I'll hide with outward squeaks
Of "meesa," "yousa," and "exquize me, sir."
So shall the simple lead the high and wise,
That all of us may dwell in harmony.

QUI-GON   I prithee, Jar Jar, how much farther on?   95

JAR JAR   We gowee underwater, kayee?
But hearee mya warning, too, sir:
De Gungans likee not outsiduhs.
De welcome may not be so warmee.

OBI-WAN   Ha! Fear thou not. This has not been a day   100
Made for the warmth of hospitality.
                    [Jar Jar leads the Jedi to the water's edge,
                    where they plunge in and swim to Gunga City.

Enter GUNGANS, *including* CAPTAIN TARPALS.

JAR JAR   Now meesa home, so good it feelee.
                    [The Gungans begin to shrink back at the
                    approach of Qui-Gon, Obi-Wan, and Jar Jar.

TARPALS   Hey yousa, stoppa there. What brings you here?

JAR JAR   Heyo-dalee, good Captain Tarpals.

TARPALS   Nay, Jar Jar, not again. Now yousa shall   105
Go to de bosses. Yousa in it deep.
                    [Captain Tarpals steps forward and prods
                    Jar Jar with his power pole, zapping him.

JAR JAR   How wude indeedee. Aye, how wudee!

TARPALS   Now commee all with me, to see de boss.
                    [Captain Tarpals and other Gungans escort Qui-Gon,
                    Obi-Wan, and Jar Jar into the chamber of the bosses.

Enter BOSS NASS *and other* GUNGAN BOSSES.

NASS   I bid to yousa welcome, gentlemen.
              But yousa cannah be here. Dis array   110
              Of mackineeks above is yous weesong.
              Dey are your problemee, not oursa, nay.
QUI-GON   An army all compris'd of droids shall soon
              Make their attack upon the kind Naboo.
              We must give them a warning, with your aid.   115
NASS   But meesa do not likee the Naboo.
              Dey think dey are so wise and full of wit.
OBI-WAN   The moment that the battle droids have done
              With the Naboo, they shall descend into
              These murky depths and seize control of you.   120
NASS   But meesa nowa thinkee so. De droids
              Not know of ussen ere.
OBI-WAN   —Have you no eyes?
              Is enmity so strong it makes you blind?
              You two—the Gungans and Naboo—do form
              A circle symbiont. The rock that's thrown   125
              Into your lake makes waves upon their shores;
              The quake that shakes their land doth make your
                                                              own
              Dear city move as though 'twere rock'd by giants.
              The same sun shines upon you both, the same
              Rain falls and bringeth water to each one,   130
              The plant that takes root in your miry depths
              Doth spread its leaves above, for them to see.
              Your fate is theirs and, aye, their fate is yours.
JAR JAR   [*aside:*] This Jedi speaketh with a wisdom keen.
NASS   But weesa do no care 'bout de Naboo.   135

[Qui-Gon uses a Jedi mind trick on Boss Nass.

QUI-GON	In that case, prithee, speed us on our way.
NASS	Yea, meesa gonna speed you bote away.
QUI-GON	And we shall have the need for transport, too.
NASS	And weesa gonna give you una bongo.
	The speedies' way to get to de Naboo 140
	Is going tru de planet core. Now, hence!
QUI-GON	With gratitude we give thee thanks, Boss Nass,
	And leave your worthy court with wish of peace.

[Qui-Gon and Obi-Wan turn to leave.

OBI-WAN	Say, Master, what doth "una bongo" mean?
QUI-GON	Methinks it is a transport. So hope I! 145
JAR JAR	[*aside:*] 'Tis now or ne'er if I would join their cause.
	[*To Qui-Gon:*] O, deysa settin' you up, certain.
	Go to de planet core? Bad bombin'.
	And any help 'ere would be hot. Eh?
OBI-WAN	Time runneth short, my master. Shall we go? 150
QUI-GON	A navigator who shall guide us through
	The planet core would be most useful, aye?
	[*To Nass:*] What shall become of this one—
	Jar Jar Binks?
NASS	Hisen to havee punishment severe.
QUI-GON	Yet I did save his life, and oweth he 155
	A debt of life to me in recompense.
	Your gods have given Jar Jar o'er to me,
	He shall go with me by divine command.
NASS	Binks? Yousen hava lifeplay witha his?
JAR JAR	O yassa, meesa doee, bossa. 160
NASS	Ah, fie! Be gone wit him. Good riddance, den.
JAR JAR	Ahh, nay, count me right outta dis here.
	'Tis betta dead here den at de core.

O whatta meesa speaka? Commink!
[Exeunt Boss Nass, Gungan bosses, and other Gungans.
      Qui-Gon, Obi-Wan, and Jar Jar enter the transport.

OBI-WAN   And now we venture to the planet core.   165
              A place most dangerous, it doth beseem.

JAR JAR   O, dis is nutsen. [*Looking out of the vessel:*]
                                            Gooberfish, O!

OBI-WAN   Why wert thou banish'd, Jar Jar? Prithee, tell.

JAR JAR   [*aside:*] If I could tell them true, they'd not believe.
              For who would think that simple-minded Binks   170
              Would come to have such thoughts expansive as
              Could threaten e'en the Gungan bosses, eh?
              O well do I recall how they assess'd
              The strange beliefs that I'd begun to speak:
              That Gungans and Naboo had equal strength,   175
              That we did need them e'en as they need us,
              That our two races should not hostile be,
              That our best future lay as one, not two.
              Such thoughts as these were reprehensible
              To all the bosses: thus, my banishment.   180
              Yet this is not the story I'll relate.
              [*To Obi-Wan:*] O issa longa tale you seeuh,
              But small part bein' meesa clumsy.

OBI-WAN   Thou wert in exile for thy clumsiness?

JAR JAR   Ahh, yousa mighten beeyuh say dat.   185

                    Enter OPEE, *hidden.*

OPEE   My lord, Darth Sidious, hath sent me here,
              Across the galaxy to help destroy
              These wretched Jedi. O, what pleasure shall

It give me—not just to fulfill the will
Of my great master, nay, but there is more   190
My villainous assignment also doth
Bring with it promise of a supper rich!
The best employment bringeth one enjoyment.

JAR JAR   [*to Obi-Wan:*] So maybe meesa causa one or,
           Uh, maybe twowee axidentee.   195
           I boom de gasser, den I banish'd.
                   [*The opee catches the transport with its tongue.*
           O nay, O nay, O dissa trouble!

                   Enter SANDO AQUA MONSTER, *aside.*

SANDO   Fear not, my Jedi brothers, for I come!
           Sent by the Jedi Council to Naboo
           To guard the good Republic's interest,   200
           My post is in the groaning waters blue
           Where I do stand a'ready to protect
           Their passage through the planet's vicious core.
           And now my chance hath come to save their lives:
           Though I am sando aqua monster call'd,   205
           I am not monstrous, nay, but virtuous.
                   [*The sando aqua monster eats the opee and exits.*
QUI-GON   Deep in the sea 'tis true, as 'tis in life:
           One fish seems vast, as giant as a fish
           Was e'er thought possible to be. We fear,
           Nay cower, in its presence, for we think   210
           It doth portend our sure and certain death.
           Now, whether 'tis a fish most literal,
           The like of which our ship has just escap'd
           Here, or, belike, 'tis but some metaphor—

	E'en some great challenge or some enemy,	215
	Mayhap some test that we must overcome—	
	Unless we call upon the Force to see	
	Correctly, that the thing is not so grand,	
	Know this: you ever shall live life in fear.	
	Hence, my young Padawan, and Jar Jar Binks,	220
	E'er bear in mind this plain and vital truth—	
	Remember that you must have confidence	
	Enough to know: there's e'er a bigger fish.	
JAR JAR	O, meesa tink we goin' back now.	
	But whereuh weesa goin' to, sir?	225
QUI-GON	Fret not: we shall be guided by the Force.	
JAR JAR	O, maxibig, de Force you sayuh.	
	But datta smella stinkowiffee.	

[The console begins to beep.

OBI-WAN   Alas, the power swiftly runneth out.
JAR JAR   O nay, O weesa die in heeyuh!   230
QUI-GON   Pray, calm thyself. No trouble have we yet.
JAR JAR   What "yet"? De monsters swimmin' out dere,
            All leakin' and a'sinkin' heeyuh,
            When yousa tinkin' we in trouble?

            Enter COLO CLAW, *hidden.*

COLO   My brother opee fail'd where I'll succeed.   235
            This vessel shall become my banquet feast—
            And thus I serve my masters by my belly.
OBI-WAN   The power is restor'd—with it, our chance.
                    [The lights of the transport turn on to reveal
                    the colo claw, which attempts to eat the ship.
QUI-GON   From one great trial to another, yet
            I feel as though some hand doth guide us here.   240

Enter SANDO AQUA MONSTER *as the transport dodges the* COLO CLAW.

SANDO   I come again to rescue my brave friends!
            Flee twixt my teeth, but you—O, colo brute!—
            Are not so fortunate. Feel my sharp bite:
            I'll break my fast upon your trait'rous hide!
                            [The sando aqua monster eats
                                the colo claw and exits.
QUI-GON   Thus are we safe again—head for that slope—   245
            For with the Force no sea may sink our hope.
                                            [Exeunt.

SCENE 4.

Aboard the Trade Federation battleship.

Enter NUTE GUNRAY, RUNE HAAKO, *and, in beam,* DARTH SIDIOUS.

NUTE   Th'invasion doth proceed apace, my lord.

SIDIOUS   I have, with cunning, slow'd the Senate's speed,
         Arresting—by procedure—their advance.
         They shall have little choice but to accept
         The strong control you hold o'er small Naboo.   5

NUTE   The queen has faith—misguided, to be sure—
         And doth believe the Senate sides with her.

SIDIOUS   Queen Amidala's but an ingénue;
         Controlling her shall not be difficult.

NUTE   Indeed, my lord.

                   [Exit Darth Sidious from beam.

RUNE   —One thing you did omit.   10
         Naught of the missing Jedi did you speak.

NUTE   Why give him reason to make loud retort?
         We shall report when we have some report.

                           [Exeunt.

SCENE 5.

On the planet Naboo.

Enter QUI-GON JINN, OBI-WAN KENOBI, *and* JAR JAR BINKS *in
transport, surfacing in the waters of Naboo.*

QUI-GON   Our journey through the core is made at last,
         And now shall we make way unto the queen

To warn her of this threat most imminent.
Come, Obi-Wan and Jar Jar, let us hence!

                                                    [Exeunt.

Enter NUTE GUNRAY *and* RUNE HAAKO *with several*
BATTLE DROIDS, *including* OOM-9.

OOM-9   The queen hath been detainèd, Viceroy.
NUTE   —Good.   5
             This victory doth taste most succulent,
             And sates the hunger of my wide ambition.

Enter SABÉ *dressed as Queen Amidala,* SIO BIBBLE,
CAPTAIN PANAKA, PADMÉ, *and other members of the*
NABOO COURT, *guarded by* BATTLE DROIDS.

SIO   How shalt thou hope to justify this bold
             Attack upon our peaceful planet? Speak!
NUTE   The queen and I shall sign a treaty soon;   10
             It shall confer legitimacy on
             Our occupation of the city here.
             I have been told the Senate shall with haste
             Proceed to ratify the treaty. Aye,
             Methinks the queen shall find it in her heart   15
             To move her hand and make the needed mark
             That shall deliver her dear populace.
SABÉ   No treaty shall I sign. You shall not have
             Cooperation in this matter—nay.
NUTE   Be sensible, Your Highness, else we shall   20
             Persuade you through the suff'ring of Naboo.
             The cries most piteous, the horrid groans,

The gleam of bodkin's touch and scream of pain,
The agony that comes from torture cruel—
These moments bleak shall have sway o'er your will.   25
[*To OOM-9:*] And now, Commander, take and
                              process them.

OOM-9   I prithee, Captain, take them to camp four.

DROID   Forsooth! Forsooth!
                  [*Exeunt Nute Gunray and Rune Haako.*

     Enter QUI-GON JINN, OBI-WAN KENOBI, *and* JAR JAR BINKS
                     above, on balcony.

QUI-GON   —The queen—now is the time!

OBI-WAN   The Force we leap withal, for victory!
          [*Qui-Gon, Obi-Wan, and Jar Jar leap down and
                 begin fighting the battle droids.*

QUI-GON   [*aside, whilst fighting:*] O, with what ease these
                       droids defeated are,   30
Had they but any skill in combat we
Would certain be outnumber'd, yet with such
A lack of acumen, these droids are no
More frightening than if they were but toys.
              [*The Jedi destroy the battle droids.*
[*To Sabé:*] Your Highness, 'twould be best to leave
                      the streets. 35

PANAKA   Ye courtiers, take the weapons of the droids!

JAR JAR   O wowsa, yousa guys so bombad.
            [*The group moves aside, off the street.*

QUI-GON   We are ambassadors and were sent here
By our wise chancellor.

SIO   —Ambassador,

	Your effort at negotiation fail'd.	40
	If I were you, a new trade would I ply.	
QUI-GON	Nay, by a Jedi's oath, there never were	
	Negotiations—only violence.	
	'Tis urgent, now, that we make contact with	
	The brave Republic. Time runs quickly out.	45
PANAKA	Communication means have been destroy'd.	
QUI-GON	But what of transport? Is there some nearby?	
PANAKA	Within the hangar—follow me anon!	

                        [The group walks to the hangar,
                                  revealing more battle droids.

	Alas, too many enemies therein;	
	Like evil thoughts these droids do multiply.	50
QUI-GON	'Twill be no problem for we Jedi two,	
	The weak shall be o'ercome by those more skill'd.	
	[To Sabé:] Your Highness, prithee journey with we two	
	To Coruscant. Belike you will be safe	
	And may before the Senate plead your cause.	55
SABÉ	With gratitude I greet your proffer'd aid,	
	Yet rightfully my place is on Naboo.	
QUI-GON	Yet they shall take your life should you remain.	
SIO	Nay, surely they would never be so bold!	
PANAKA	They need the queen to sign their treaty, so	60
	To render this invasion legal. Should	
	They kill her, they would lose their one defense.	
QUI-GON	And yet I sense there may be more at play:	
	What game's afoot is still a mystery,	
	No logic guides the Federation's moves.	65
	My feeling is: they mean to do you harm.	
	I would not have a queen become a pawn.	
SIO	Our only hope is for the Senate's help.	

	The senator, e'en Palpatine, shall need
	Your good assistance in this matter, ma'am. 70
SABÉ	This situation grave is dangerous.
	[*To Padmé:*] Aye, dangerous for all who shall go forth.
PADMÉ	Yet we are brave, Your Highness. We shall go.
QUI-GON	If you would leave, Your Highness, 'twill be now.
SABÉ	Enough, I am engag'd. I'll challenge this, 75
	And venture forth to plead my case before
	The Senate. Hope shall be our strength and stay.

[*They begin walking toward the transport.*

Enter BATTLE DROIDS *guarding* PILOTS, *including* RIC OLIÉ.

PANAKA	The pilots must be freed if we would fly.
OBI-WAN	'Twould be my joy to free them of their bonds.

[*Obi-Wan makes his way toward the pilots as
Qui-Gon is stopped by a guard droid.*

DROID	Desist at once, and take no further step. 80
QUI-GON	I am the chancellor's ambassador.
	I tell thee I must take these people here
	To Coruscant.
DROID	—Well, where shalt thou take them?
QUI-GON	To Coruscant, thou brute.
DROID	—Why, you shall take
	Them, then, to Coruscant. Alack, this doth 85
	Go 'gainst my programming, doth not compute!
	Behold, I place you all under arrest.
QUI-GON	Thou shalt a ghost droid be ere I am through.

[*Qui-Gon destroys guard droid with his lightsaber.
Obi-Wan destroys droids guarding pilots. Sabé, Padmé,
and Captain Panaka begin to board transport.*

PANAKA   Anon, we fly!

OBI-WAN   —Ye pilots all, make haste!

                [The pilots run to various vessels. Ric Olié boards the
                    queen's transport with Qui-Gon and Obi-Wan.

RIC   It is my duty and mine honor to   90

            Protect and serve the queen whom I adore!

                      [The ship flies off. Exeunt.

      Enter OBI-WAN KENOBI *and* JAR JAR BINKS *aside in ship, with*
      ASTROMECH DROIDS *including* R2-D2.

OBI-WAN   Pray, stay thou here and mischief do thou none.

                      [Exit Obi-Wan.

JAR JAR   Heigh-ho, my lads. Are ye misunderstood

            As Jar Jar Binks and his dear Gungans? Eh?

            Know ye of human prejudice and scorn?   95

            Methinks ye must, as all nonhumans do.

                      [Exit Jar Jar.

      Enter QUI-GON JINN, OBI-WAN KENOBI, CAPTAIN PANAKA,
        and RIC OLIÉ *in cockpit.*

RIC   The blockade doth appear, to work us woe.

            They shoot at us, and we are sorely hit!

            The generator of the shield is down.

            Mayhap this doth betoken our defeat!   100

                  [Astromech droids move outside the ship
                    to repair the shield generator.

R2-D2   Beep, meep, beep, squeak, beep, whistle, meep,

                      meep, hoo!

            [Aside:] It is my time to serve and prove my worth!

            I would the brave Republic serve with pride,

            For I do long for some advent'rous life,

With galaxies to see and quests to take,   105
And even more: I long to be inspir'd
And join a noble cause to which I may
Contribute all my strength and skill and wit.
Now to it, R2, serve thy very best!
                    [Several astromech droids are destroyed
                              by fire from the blockade.

OBI-WAN   Alas, these droids do fall like winter snow,   110
Each flake snuff'd out by flaming sword of fire.
We soon shall have no more, and then we're lost.

PANAKA   Without the generator we are dead—
The shots shall find their mark and end our lives.

RIC   The shields are gone. 'Tis done, my comrades. Done!   115

R2-D2   Beep, meep, beep, hoo!

RIC   —But O, what sign is this?
The power hath return'd, and with it, too,
Our prospect of survival. O, hurrah!
The droid hath done the deed; he bypass'd the
Main power drive. Deflector shields are up   120
To maximum effect, and we are sav'd.
                    [R2-D2 returns inside the ship.
One thing remains, however, worthy friends:
There ship hath not not sufficient power to
Deliver us to Coruscant. It is
The hyperdrive, it leaketh out, like blood   125
From some deep wound within its metal core.

QUI-GON   We must make landing to repair, refuel.
No ship is shipshape sans a solid structure.

OBI-WAN   [*consulting star charts:*] Look, Master, here is
                                        found a planet near.
I have not heard its name: 'tis Tatooine.   130

'Tis small and poor, and far from ev'rything;
The Federation hath no presence there.

PANAKA   What confidence have you in this remark?

QUI-GON   The planet is controllèd by the Hutts.

PANAKA   The Hutts, indeed. Such lowly gangsters of   135
Base reputation, fill'd with avarice:
Their minds on money, money on their minds.
Such lowly, wormlike villainy as theirs
No royalty should e'er bear witness to,
Or forcèd be to find the strength t'endure.   140
O nay, ye Jedis, find another course:
Pray, let us not take her to Tatooine!

QUI-GON   E'en if they did discover her, 'twould be
No diff'rent than if our lame ship were bound
For any place the Federation holds.   145
Except, my friend: the Hutts expect her not,
Nor are they searching for the noble queen.
We do, then, have a strong advantage here—
Thus let us land, with hopefulness sincere.

[Exeunt.

SCENE 1.

Aboard the Trade Federation battleship.

Enter NUTE GUNRAY, RUNE HAAKO, *and, in beam,* DARTH SIDIOUS.

SIDIOUS	My patience runneth out, so tell me true:
	Hath Amidala sign'd the treaty yet?
NUTE	My lord, with trepidation I report:
	The queen hath disappear'd. There was one ship
	From small Naboo escap'd our stout blockade.
SIDIOUS	That treaty shall be sign'd! I will it so.
NUTE	But 'tis impossible to find the ship.
	It lies beyond our range of scope or measure.

5

Enter DARTH MAUL *in beam with* DARTH SIDIOUS.

SIDIOUS   For thy weak instruments, perhaps, but not,
            I tell thee truly, Viceroy, for a Sith.   10
            Behold my Sith apprentice: Darth Maul he.
            Your lost ship shall be swiftly found by him.
                                [Exeunt Darth Sidious and
                                    Darth Maul from beam.

NUTE   Oft double is a thing that one would wish:
            A double blessing is a boon, indeed,
            A double meaning renders one word two,   15
            A double-edgèd sword may cut both ways,
            A double honor is a monarch's gift.
            But what is this when evil doubl'd is?
            'Tis then that one hath trouble doubl'd, too.

RUNE   This deal is one that we should have declin'd,   20
            For now we two are in a double bind.
                                                [Exeunt.

SCENE 2.
Aboard the Naboo cruiser.

Enter QUI-GON JINN, OBI-WAN KENOBI, SABÉ *dressed as*
Queen Amidala, CAPTAIN PANAKA, PADMÉ, *and* R2-D2.

PANAKA   The hero of our quick escape is here:
            This little droid, so well and deftly made.
            Sans doubt it sav'd the ship and our own lives.

SABÉ   The droid shall have my royal commendation.
            What is the droidly number it doth bear?   5

PANAKA	'Tis R2-D2, Highness.
SABÉ	—All our thanks
	And gratitude we bear to thee, good droid:
	Thou brave and gallant R2-D2.
R2-D2	—Beep!
SABÉ	Pray, Padmé, clean this droid with all thy skill.
	It is deserving of what kindness we 10
	May proffer to it.
R2-D2	—Meep, beep, whistle, squeak!

[Padmé and R2-D2 move aside
and she begins cleaning the droid.

SABÉ	Continue with thy briefing, Captain, please.
PANAKA	I call on Jedi Qui-Gon Jinn to speak.
QUI-GON	Your Highness, with permission we shall fly
	Unto a planet small call'd Tatooine. 15
	It lieth in a system far beyond
	The Federation's harsh and grasping reach.
PANAKA	The Jedi's will and mine do not agree.
QUI-GON	I prithee, trust my judgment, Highness. Let
	My wisdom make its proof by worthy deeds. 20

[Exeunt Qui-Gon, Obi-Wan,
Sabé, and Captain Panaka.

Enter JAR JAR BINKS.

JAR JAR	Hello! Say whosa are-a yousa?
PADMÉ	I'm Padmé call'd, handmaiden to the queen.
JAR JAR	And meesa Jar Jar Binks, dass meesa.
PADMÉ	Thou art a Gungan, art thou not? 'Tis true?
JAR JAR	[*aside:*] O, she is swift of mind. "A Gungan," ha! 25
	Her thoughts already label me as brute.

PADMÉ   How didst thou come to be on board with us?

JAR JAR   [*aside:*] And wherefore doth she ask? A ship, belike,
             Is no place for a Gungan to be found.
             She would assume we lurk in swamp and mire,   30
             Not in her precious folly-laden ship.
             But soft you, Jar Jar, give the girl your best.
             [*To Padmé:*] Ahh, me no know. Me daysa startin'
             So okeeday with brisky mornin'
             A'munchen. Den de boomy boomy,   35
             And meesa scardee, grabbin' Jedi,
             Then powsa, meesa wit you heera.
             Now meesa gettin' very scardee.

PADMÉ   Indeed, this is a day for fear and doubt—
             It seems your cause and mine are well align'd.   40

                         [*Exeunt Jar Jar and Padmé.*]

        Enter QUI-GON JINN, OBI-WAN KENOBI, CAPTAIN PANAKA,
                    and RIC OLIÉ *in cockpit.*

RIC   'Tis there, below! The planet Tatooine.

OBI-WAN   Our scope doth show a settlement nearby.

QUI-GON   Land thou the ship beyond its boundary.
             I would not seek more notice than we need.

                         [*Exeunt Captain Panaka and Ric Olié.*]

OBI-WAN   The generator of the hyperdrive   45
             Is done and finish'd, Master. We shall need
             To make repair ere we depart from here.

QUI-GON   This is a complication to our plans.
             And there is more: I pray, be on thy guard:
             I sense a great disturbance in the Force.   50

OBI-WAN   I feel it also, Master. 'Tis as if

Some evil is arising in our midst.

QUI-GON   Be certain that they no transmissions make.
            I shall go forth to find a hyperdrive
            That shall suffice to make the ship's repair.   55
            Stay thou behind, her Highness to defend.

                                        [Exit Qui-Gon.

OBI-WAN   Now wherefore am I left to watch the ship
            When I too am a Jedi, just as he?
            Nay, still my tongue—'tis not for me to guess
            At my wise master's thoughts, or criticize.   60
            My master Qui-Gon is a pow'rful man
            And hath been more than teacher unto me.
            Full fortunate am I—and well I know't—
            To be the man's apprentice. Many would
            Consider such a post and master more   65
            Than any Jedi should expect. Indeed,
            To be with Qui-Gon is to be well serv'd
            By the uncertain, fickle hand of Fate.
            I shall be dutiful till he come back,
            And keep the queen protected from attack.   70

                                        [Exit.

SCENE 3.

On the planet Tatooine.

Enter QUI-GON JINN, JAR JAR BINKS, *and* R2-D2.

QUI-GON   Come, Jar Jar, let us find the settlement.
JAR JAR   Dis sun is murther for me skinnee.

Enter CAPTAIN PANAKA *and* PADMÉ.

PANAKA	Kind sirs, a word! The queen doth wish for you
	To take her handmaiden along with you.
QUI-GON	No more commands shall we obey today; 5
	Her Highness hath already had her fill.
	The spaceport we make expedition t'ward
	Is not some royal court: it shall be rife
	With fearsome, base, and vicious characters.
	It is no place to bring a handmaiden. 10
PANAKA	The queen desires it; curious is she
	About this planet and what lies hereon.
QUI-GON	This is a course with which I disagree:
	A queen's desire's not rationale enough.
	[*To Padmé:*] Remain close at my side. I'll see thee
	safe. 15

[*Exit Captain Panaka as Qui-Gon, Padmé,*
Jar Jar, and R2-D2 walk toward the spaceport.

PADMÉ	What know you of this land, this Tatooine?
	Who are its people, what is their employ?
QUI-GON	'Tis modest moisture farmers, in the main.
	Some tribes indigenous, and scavengers.
	The spaceports such as this are haven to 20
	Those who aren't lost, and yet would not be found.
PADMÉ	Indeed, your words describe our company.
JAR JAR	O dissen veree veree baddee.
QUI-GON	Let us seek out a smaller dealer here—
	More likely shall we then be unobserv'd. 25

Enter WATTO.

WATTO   Oo ditta noya? Chuba di naya?

QUI-GON   Strange flying imp, I do require parts for
           A J-type three-two-seven Nubian.

WATTO   Aye, Nubian, our strong specifically.
           We have full many of those parts herein.   30
           [*To Anakin, within:*] Peedunkel! Naba dee unko!

QUI-GON   —My droid
           Doth carry all the details technical.

           Enter ANAKIN SKYWALKER.

WATTO   [*to Anakin:*] Coona tee-tocky malia, peedunk'?

ANAKIN	Mel tassa cholpassa. [*Aside:*] My master asks
	What kept me, yet did I not come anon? 35
WATTO	Chut! Ganda doe wallya. Me dwana n'bat'.
	[*To Qui-Gon:*] The boy shall watch the store,
	whilst we discourse
	Your needs—belike the part outside awaits.
	I prithee, thither come with me, my friend.
QUI-GON	[*to Jar Jar:*] Thou fool: touch nothing, lest thou
	mischief make. 40
	[*Qui-Gon and Watto walk aside.*
ANAKIN	[*aside:*] Though I am young, and burden'd by the shine
	Of too much sunlight here on Tatooine,
	Still I can tell the presence of a light
	Far brighter than e'er I dream'd possible.
	O, she doth teach the torches to burn bright! 45
	[*To Padmé:*] Excuse me this intrusion, madam, but:
	Are you by some celestial body sent?
	Did you make home beyond the galaxy,
	Whence you did come to bless my little life?
PADMÉ	What didst thou say?
ANAKIN	—Are you celesti'lly born? 50
	Those pilots who do wander deep in space
	Do tell of beings pure and undefil'd:
	Such beauty's in their aspect and their song
	That all who hear their music 'gin to weep
	And long to be forever in the sway 55
	Of their most splendid, perfect melody.
	Methinks they live upon the moon Iego,
	And there they play their notes for all who pass.
PADMÉ	Thou art a droll, audacious little boy.
	How comes this knowledge from such youthful lips? 60

ANAKIN   I do but listen: train my ear toward
             The traders and the pilots who traverse
             This lonely planet. Truly, I do call
             Myself a pilot, too, and shall one day
             Fly far beyond this planet's stifling reach.   65

PADMÉ   Thou art a pilot?

ANAKIN   —Troth, for all the days
             I have upon this barren planet dwell'd.

PADMÉ   What is the number of those days thereon?

ANAKIN   O, since I was a lad of but three years.
             My mother and myself were peddl'd to   70
             Gardulla of the Hutt, who did but lose
             Her new investment gambling o'er the pods.

PADMÉ   Thou art a slave?

ANAKIN   —O appellation dire!
             Pray, when you think of me think not of slave.
             Think not that I am baseborn, made to work,   75
             Think not of one who lives by harsh commands,
             Think not of one whose destiny's controll'd,
             Think rather of my worthy qualities,
             Think of my name, good lady: Anakin.

PADMÉ   And so I shall, hereafter. Pardon me,   80
             For I do not full understanding have
             Of this strange place, which is still new to me.
                         *[Jar Jar touches a small droid, which
                                 begins to walk around and break
                                 things. Jar Jar seizes the droid.*

ANAKIN   O silly beast, strike it upon the nose!
                         *[Jar Jar touches the small droid's
                                 nose, and it collapses.*

WATTO   [*aside with Qui-Gon:*] The generator for the hyperdrive

For your T-14 . . . ahh, methinks 'tis close!   85
Fate smiles on you today: I am, nearby,
The sole possessive of the needed part.
You would do well to purchase some new ship,
For mayhap 'twould be cheaper so to do.
And since we do of money start to speak,   90
How shall you pay for this extensive part?

QUI-GON   I have some twenty thousand in my store—
Dactaries, the Republic's tender true.

WATTO   Republic credits? You are misaligned:
On Tatooine your credits are no use.   95

QUI-GON   [attempting a Jedi mind trick:] I've nothing else,
                                    but credits shall suffice.

WATTO   Nay, they shall not.
QUI-GON   —Aye, credits shall suffice.

WATTO   Do you not compromise? Do you believe
Yourself to be a Jedi, who, with but
A wave of your sly hand, may change my mind?   100
I am Toydarian, and proudly so;
Your mind decapitations touch not me,
'Tis only money moves my cunning mind.
No currency is but no parts, no parts
Is but no deal, no deal is noisome; thus,   105
I shall depart unsatisfi'd from thee.
And more, no other merchant can provide
The hyperdrive for your fail'd T-14.
Of that, good man, I give you conflagration.
             [Qui-Gon turns to leave, walking back toward
                           Jar Jar, Padmé, and Anakin.

ANAKIN   [to Padmé:] These droids enjoy more life than
                                    they are due,   110

	Which is—to speak my strength—due to my skill.
QUI-GON	We must depart. If't please you, follow on.
ANAKIN	[*aside:*] So quickly met and then so quickly lost?
PADMÉ	'Twas well that I did meet thee, Anakin.
ANAKIN	The joy was mine, good lady, fare you well. 115

ANAKIN   [*Aside:*] O, we must meet again, else my heart's lost!
                              [*Exeunt Watto and Anakin.*

QUI-GON   [*into communicator:*] Good Obi-Wan, I bid thee,
                              hear my words:
                 Doth our small ship have aught of value in't?

Enter OBI-WAN KENOBI *on balcony, in ship.*

OBI-WAN   We have some few containers with supplies.
                 The queen's exquisite wardrobe, mayhap, yet   120
                 'Tis not so much as would a barter serve,
                 Not if you do require a handsome sum.
QUI-GON   'Tis well enough. A different result
                 May from another quarter come. Adieu.
                              [*Exit Obi-Wan.*
JAR JAR   Nowotha. Beings here cawayzee.   125
                 Now weesa will be robb'd and crunchee.
R2-D2   Beep, meep, beep, squeak! [*Aside:*] I'll warrant
                              Jar Jar hath
                 More in his Gungan head than it doth seem.
QUI-GON   It is unlikely—sure, what would they rob?
                 We have no assets: trouble's all we own.   130
JAR JAR   [*aside:*] I shall make some distraction for us here,
                 Perchance from chaos, order may arise.
                              [*Walking past a café, Jar Jar strikes a piece
                              of meat with his tongue as Qui-Gon, Padmé,*

and R2-D2 continue on.

Enter VENDOR *and, aside,* SEBULBA.

VENDOR   Eh, eh, na wanna wunga? Tenga wup'!
          [Jar Jar releases the meat, which hits Sebulba.
             Sebulba moves to Jar Jar, striking him.
SEBULBA   E chuba nai?

Enter ANAKIN SKYWALKER.

ANAKIN   [*aside:*] —My newfound friend needs help,
         Else vile Sebulba shall do him some harm.   135
         I shall report this Gungan is someone
         Of great import, and quick to anger, too.
         Thus may he live. [*To Sebulba:*] Chess ko, Sebulba,
                                         aye.
         Cha porko ootman geesa. Me teesa
         Rodda co pana pee choppa chawa.   140
SEBULBA   Neek me chawa, wermo, mo killee ma
         Klounkee. Un' notu wo shag, m'wompity
         Du pom pom.
                [Exeunt Sebulba and vendor.
ANAKIN   —O, how roguish is this one!
         He saith he shall make my sure defeat
         When next we meet again, and would destroy   145
         Me now, would Watto not a young slave lose.
         His words I fear not, though he speaks them rough.
               [Qui-Gon, Padmé, and R2-D2 return.
         Well met, my friends. Your odd companion was
         Beset by trouble most severe, and would

	Have forfeited his life, for nearly did 150

Have forfeited his life, for nearly did   150
He come to fisticuffs, e'en with a Dug—
A vicious one—Sebulba is his name.

JAR JAR   O meesa haten crunchee, issa
De last thing meesa wantin' heera.

QUI-GON   And yet, the boy is right. Thou courtest trouble.   155
[*To Anakin:*] With gratitude I thank thee, little friend.

JAR JAR   But what? For meesa doin' nothin'. . .

ANAKIN   Pray, come with me, and try these pallies here.
                    [*Anakin purchases a confection from a vendor.*

QUI-GON   I do accept, with thanks.

ANAKIN   [*aside:*]   —But what is this
I spy as he doth turn aside his cloak?   160
A Jedi's weapon!—I shall know more of't.
[*To Qui-Gon:*] A storm of sand arises soon, my liege:
Do you have ample shelter from the squall?

QUI-GON   We shall return anon unto our ship.

ANAKIN   But is it far?

PADMÉ   —'Tis on the outskirts. Why?   165

ANAKIN   [*aside:*] Ahh, just the turn of chance for which I
                                        hop'd—
An opportunity to see her more.
[*To Padmé:*] You never shall the outskirts reach in time;
Such storms on Tatooine may deadly be.
Consider your fine party honor'd guests   170
In my most humble home. 'Tis not too far.
            [*The company makes its way to Anakin's house
                    as the sandstorm begins to blow.*
Fond mother, mother dear, art thou herein?

Enter SHMI SKYWALKER.

SHMI	Indeed; here I do stand.
ANAKIN	—These are my friends.
R2-D2	Beep, whistle, squeak!
QUI-GON	—My name is Qui-Gon Jinn.

Your son did kindly offer shelter here.   175

ANAKIN [*to Padmé:*] I spend my moments free within my

                                                            room,

Engag'd in such pursuits as droid design.

Pray, thither come, and Threepio you'll meet.

PADMÉ Lead on, I follow.

[Exeunt Qui-Gon, Shmi, and Jar Jar.
Padmé, Anakin, and R2-D2 walk aside,
to his chamber. Anakin reveals C-3PO.

ANAKIN	—'Tis C-3PO!
	Is he not something wondrous to behold? 180
	The droid is not yet finish'd, but is close.
PADMÉ	Indeed, the droid is sign and testament
	To your vast skill and ingenuity.
R2-D2	[*aside:*] A scan doth show the droid is finely made—
	In time, perchance, I'll know him better still. 185
ANAKIN	He is a droid of protocol, design'd
	To help my kindly mother in her work.
	Behold, and see him animate with life!

                                       [Anakin turns on C-3PO.

C-3PO	C-3PO am I, an expert in
	The human-cyborg link. How may I serve? 190
PADMÉ	He is perfection, Anakin.
C-3PO	—Am I?
ANAKIN	When this dark storm subsideth, I shall show
	My racer unto you—for racing pods.
C-3PO	[*walking:*] This floor may not entirely stable be.
	[*To R2-D2:*] My greetings, for we've not been
	introduc'd. 195
R2-D2	Beep, meep, beep, beep, meep, whistle, beep,
	meep, squeak.
C-3PO	'Tis R2-D2, aye? A pleasure, sir.
	C-3PO am I, an expert in
	The human-cyborg link.
R2-D2	—Beep, whistle, woo?
C-3PO	I beg your pardon, droid—what do you mean 200
	When that you call me "naked," impish one?
R2-D2	Beep, whistle, beep!
C-3PO	—My parts are all reveal'd?
	My parts are not so starkly bare as your

Impolitic assertion, naughty droid.
My protocol is tested by this scene.   205

Enter Obi-Wan Kenobi, Sabé *dressed as Queen Amidala,*
Captain Panaka, *and* Sio Bibble *in beam, on balcony.*

SIO   The Federation hath cut off supply
Of food until you make return. And more,
The death toll hath been catastrophic here.
Conform unto their wishes, Highness, please,
And contact me anon, ere more are dead.   210
[Exit Sio Bibble from beam.

OBI-WAN   'Tis but a ruse, Your Highness, take no mind.
Send no reply—transmissions make ye none.
[Exeunt Sabé and Captain Panaka from balcony.
[*Into communicator:*] Good Master, message comes
from small Naboo,
And of their situation makes report.

QUI-GON   It soundeth like some bait through which, by trick,   215
The Federation may soon trace us here.

OBI-WAN   What if it speaketh verily indeed?
What shall we do if people perish there?

QUI-GON   In either case, the sands of time run out.
[Exit Obi-Wan from balcony.

Enter Padmé, Anakin Skywalker, Shmi Skywalker,
Jar Jar Binks, *and* R2-D2.

SHMI   I bid ye sit, and we'll together sup.   220
QUI-GON   With thanks we'll share your table happily.
I prithee, tell me of your life as slave.

SHMI   All slaves are fit with small transmitters, which
            Within our bodies hidden do reside.
ANAKIN   I seek to build a scanner to find mine.   225
SHMI   If, then, a slave doth try to make escape—
ANAKIN   That slave shall make a frightful final flight.
PADMÉ   'Tis difficult to think that slavery
            Doth still exist within the galaxy.
            The good Republic hath such laws as should—   230
SHMI   Yet your Republic is but naught out here.
            On Tatooine we must survive by wits.

            *[Jar Jar snatches a piece of fruit with
            his tongue, eats it, and belches.*

JAR JAR   O beggee pardon, me excoosee.
ANAKIN   Has any one of ye a podrace seen?
QUI-GON   They have podracing o'er on Malastare.   235
            'Tis dangerous, 'tis fast and furious.
ANAKIN   Methinks I am the human lone can do't.
QUI-GON   Thou must have Jedi reflexes if so.

            *[Jar Jar attempts to snatch another piece
            of fruit and Qui-Gon catches his tongue.*

            [*To Jar Jar:*] Cease thou this rude and unbecoming

                                                            act!

ANAKIN	You are a Jedi Knight. Is not this true?	240
QUI-GON	Why wouldst thou think a thing as this, young lad?	
ANAKIN	I saw your sword bewitch'd with laser beam.	
	None but the Jedi wield such rare defense.	
QUI-GON	Perhaps I slew a Jedi, then took it.	
ANAKIN	It is not so, for I believe no one	245
	Hath pow'r enough, a Jedi for to slay.	
QUI-GON	O how I wish that such a thing were true.	
ANAKIN	I dream'd, once long ago, that I—e'en I—	
	Had train'd to be a Jedi, then return'd	
	To Tatooine to liberate each slave.	250
	'Twas but a dream, yet, O, how sweet its touch.	
	Have you, good sir, come to deliver us?	
QUI-GON	Nay, nay, unfortunately I have not.	
ANAKIN	You say 'tis so, and yet I think you wrong:	
	I do believe you have come bearing freedom.	255
	For wherefore else fly here, to Tatooine?	
QUI-GON	'Tis plain to me thou wilt not be the fool,	
	Young Anakin. We go to Coruscant,	
	The central system of th'Republic, on	
	An enterprise of great pith and moment.	260
ANAKIN	How thither came your company, e'en to	
	The Outer Rim?	
PADMÉ	—Our ship was damagèd,	
	And we are stranded till we make repair.	
ANAKIN	For certain, I shall lend you aid, for I	
	Am skill'd and can fix any broken thing.	265
QUI-GON	Indeed, I verily believe thou canst.	
	But first, we must acquire the parts we need.	
JAR JAR	We no got nutten mula tradee.	
PADMÉ	These refuse dealers must some weakness have.	

SHMI	'Tis gambling—all the commerce here doth spin, 270
	In shaky orbit, 'round the sun of those
	Most awful, frightful races—e'en the pods.
QUI-GON	Podracing, yea. O, greed an ally strong
	May be—mayhap 'tis something we can use.
ANAKIN	I built a racer—aye, the fastest e'er. 275
	A podrace happens on the morrow, e'en
	On Boonta Eve. My pod may be your wager.
SHMI	Peace, Anakin! Thou knowest Watto shall
	Not let thee enter into any race!
ANAKIN	He knoweth not that I have built the thing! 280
	You, Qui-Gon, may make him think it is yours,
	Convincing him to let me pilot it.
SHMI	I shall not see't. I die when thou dost race.
	Say, wouldst thou slay a mother's heart again?
ANAKIN	Yet, Mother, 'tis what I do love to do. 285
	The money to be made upon the course
	Would more than pay for parts of which they've need.
SHMI	Fie, Anakin . . .
QUI-GON	—Thy mother hath the right.
	Tell me, I pray: is there none friendly to
	Republic's cause who'd rise and lend us aid? 290
SHMI	Alas, there's none. Not here on Tatooine.
ANAKIN	Sweet mother, hear my words and know my heart:
	My love for you is vast beyond compare,
	You know that I love naught so well as you.
	'Tis you who taught me this: our universe 295
	Is massive, infinite. The trouble, though,
	Begins because no one shall help the other.
	A universe of beings, and each one
	Is too uncaring or afraid to stretch
	Their arms out wide and proffer helping hands. 300

Shall we, in this grim moment of their need,
Do just as others do and turn our backs?

PADMÉ   In troth, I know that Qui-Gon willingly
Would not put thy sweet son in danger's way.
Another path we somehow shall seek out.   305

SHMI   The boy is right; there is no other way.
What I desire is not the utmost here:
He may assist you in the race. Indeed,
It seemeth he was meant to meet thy need.

                                        [Exeunt.

SCENE 4.

On the planet Coruscant.

Enter RUMOR.

RUMOR   E'en as the Jedi fret to find their part,
New enemies do move to work them woe.
The Sith hath come, with evil in his heart,
Equipp'd with might to rise against his foe.
Replete with thoughts dark and insidious,   5
The Sith, Darth Sidious, doth plan his move.
He—with Darth Maul, apprentice hideous—
Expects they shall their obstacles remove.
So come they now, these men of vice and fear,
Illicitly to make all bend the knee,   10
Till they've the power, which they hold so dear,
Help'd by this Rumor through the galaxy.

                                        [Exit.

Enter DARTH SIDIOUS *and* DARTH MAUL.

MAUL   The planet Tatooine hath settlements
     But few and far between. Thus, if the trace
     Hath done its work, I shall find them anon,   15
     Good Master.

SIDIOUS   —Move against the Jedi first.
     That done, the queen thou shalt with ease convince
     To sign the treaty back in small Naboo.

MAUL   At last, we shall reveal ourselves unto
     The overcertain, pompous Jedi. Ha!   20
     At last, forsooth, we shall see our revenge.

SIDIOUS   Thou hast been trainèd well, apprentice mine;
     They shall in no wise be a match for thee.

                   [Exit Darth Sidious.

MAUL   What seeds of bitterness the Jedi sow
     By their ambition and their errant pride.   25
     Darth Sidious is god; and to his law
     My services are bound. Wherefore should I
     Stand in the plague of custom, and thus let
     The curiosity of galaxies
     Deprive me for that I am some twelve deeds   30
     Lag of some honor? Why Sith? Wherefore base?
     The path of shadows is my chosen way,
     And who shall call me "villain" for the choice?
     If 'tis some villainy to search for pow'r,
     If 'tis a sin to sing the dark side's praise,   35
     If 'tis an evil, striving 'gainst the wrong,
     If this is so, a Sith may be call'd base.
     My master with all readiness I serve,
     That I may aid the downfall of the vile,

Contemptible and tiresome Jedi Council.   40
A Sith I'll be, and to my master sworn,
And face the Jedi with mine utmost scorn.

          [Exit Darth Maul.

SCENE 5.

On the planet Tatooine.

Enter PADMÉ.

PADMÉ   How shall I silent be with this fool plan?
              A queen—and her handmaiden—should speak out.
              A queen—e'en her handmaiden—may object.
              A queen—aye, too, her handmaiden—must balk
              At this idea that hath no merit to't.   5
              So shall this maiden play her hand as 'twere
              The queen herself who doth her wishes speak.

Enter QUI-GON JINN.

              Are you convinc'd 'tis wise to trust this fate
              That weaves for us a boy we hardly know?
              The queen would not approve, if she were here.   10
QUI-GON   'Tis fortunate for us she shall not know.
PADMÉ   Yet neither doth my maiden's heart approve.

                           [Exit Padmé.

Enter WATTO *and* ANAKIN SKYWALKER.

WATTO   The boy doth say that you would speckle him

To race? How can you do this thing? Say how!
Methinks not with Republic credits, ha!   15

QUI-GON   My ship—the Nubian—shall be my fee.

WATTO   'Tis well, 'tis well.

QUI-GON   —The ship is well attir'd,
But for the parts of which I have a need.

WATTO   In what do you propose the boy would ride?
For he did smash my pod in his last race.   20
Methinks he hath not time to make repair.

ANAKIN   In troth, 'twas not my fault. Sebulba flash'd
Me with his vents. I sav'd the pod—well, most.

WATTO   Aye, this is true; the boy is deeply skill'd.

QUI-GON   Within a rough cantina close nearby,   25
I gain'd a pod a'playing games of chance.
It is the fastest ever built, they say.

WATTO   I hope you kill'd no one I know for it:
Toydarians treat homophones with care.
Yet if you do speak true, you here propose   30
To offer up the pod and entry fee,
Whilst I supply the boy. If then we win,
You shall have half and I the other, yea?

QUI-GON   If I supply two things and thou but one,
And still we split the winnings by their halves,   35
I must have some assurance: you, my friend,
Shall first provide the entry fee in cash.
Then if we win, you keep the money but
For those few parts I need. And should we lose,
You keep my ship. In either case, you win.   40

WATTO   The deal is yours—and may we have success!
                                                  [Exit Qui-Gon.
[*To Anakin:*] Yo bana pee ho-tah, meendee ya, eh?

[Exeunt Watto and Anakin.

Enter QUI-GON JINN *speaking into communicator to*
OBI-WAN KENOBI, *who enters above, on balcony.*

OBI-WAN   What if this plan doth not succeed aright?
                 It may be eons till we leave this place.

QUI-GON   To call for help is far too dangerous,   45
                 And yet, a ship sans pow'r shall not release
                 Us from this barren planet, Tatooine.
                 Moreover, there is something in this boy
                 I would discover ere we do depart.
                                   [Exit Obi-Wan from balcony.

                 Enter SHMI SKYWALKER.

SHMI   Good e'en.

QUI-GON   —Good e'en. Thou shouldst be proud of thy   50
                 Young son. He gives no thought of a reward.

SHMI   He knows no greed. He hath—how shall I say't?

QUI-GON   He hath a power most profound, 'tis true?

SHMI   Aye.

QUI-GON   —He doth see things ere they do transpire.
                 'Tis why the speed of his reflexes seems   55
                 So swift—it is a Jedi quality.

SHMI   He doth deserve more than a slaving life.

QUI-GON   Had he been born under Republic skies,
                 He would have been identified when young
                 And then become a Jedi. Yea, the Force   60
                 Is strong with him indeed, 'tis passing strong.
                 Who, prithee, was the father to the boy?

SHMI	Alas, I do not know. Mistake me not:
	View not this tale of mine with a mistrust
	Ere you have heard it all: there was no father. 65
	My boy is mine—I carried him until
	Arriv'd the very moment of his birth,
	Rais'd I the babe into the lad and yet,
	I still cannot explain how he did come.
	And now I shall ask you: can you help him? 70
QUI-GON	I do not know. In troth, I did not come
	To Tatooine to liberate its slaves.

Enter ANAKIN SKYWALKER, PADMÉ, JAR JAR BINKS,
R2-D2, C-3PO, KITSTER, SEEK, AMEE, *and* WALD,
working on Anakin's podracer.

KITSTER	A veritable astro droid! How art
	Thou e'er so fortunate, O Anakin?
ANAKIN	There's better still shall come: the Boonta race 75
	Shall be my playground on the morrow.
KITSTER	—Eh?
	With this most scrap-infested heap of bones?
WALD	Na jesko joka, Anakin, ho ho!
AMEE	Thou hast work'd on the podracer for years.
	It never shall give thou the speed thou need'st. 80
SEEK	Come, let's be gone unto some other sport.
	If he keep'st on, he will soon smashèd be.
	[Exeunt Wald, Amee, and Seek.
ANAKIN	I bid thee, Jar Jar, keep thy distance from
	The binders of vast energy thereon.
	Shouldst thou e'en get a finger caught within, 85
	Thou shalt for hours bear with its numbing pain.

JAR JAR   [*aside:*] The little master doth instruct me right,
             Yet so that he shall think me quite unwise
             I'll risk a moment in the binder's beam.

                       [*Jar Jar bends down, catching his
                            mouth in the energy binders.*

             [*To Anakin:*] My tonguee sisso rubba innee.   90
C-3PO   I find the creature Jar Jar rather odd.
R2-D2   Beep, squeak! [*Aside:*] Yet who is odder, Threepio?
KITSTER   Hear, Anakin: how canst be sure 'twill run?
ANAKIN   Have faith, good friend: the pod shall serve us well.
QUI-GON   The time hath come to test thy surety.   95
             Behold, a power source that thou mayst use.
ANAKIN   Forsooth, I shall—in every good thing!
PADMÉ   The Gungan now is caught in th'afterburner.
             I shall release him now, the silly fool.

                       [*Padmé moves to free Jar Jar as
                            Anakin starts the podracer.*

C-3PO   Indeed, the beast is odd beyond degree.   100
ANAKIN   Now, rise, you swift podracer, rise and fly!
             It comes to life beneath its master's touch—
             The fleet machine doth work, it shall succeed,
             And with it ev'ry hope that's in our hearts.

                       [*Exeunt Padmé, Jar Jar, Shmi,
                            R2-D2, and C-3PO in mirth.*

QUI-GON   An excellent a'testing of the pod,   105
             Young Anakin. Yet now I see thou hast
             Been hurt—a scratch from thy wild metal beast.
             I bid thee, sit thou here and I'll mend it.
ANAKIN   Behold the stars above, so numerous!
             So brightly do they shine upon the world   110
             That I can almost see my future by them.

	Do all have planetary systems, sir?
QUI-GON	Belike near all the stars have planets, too.
ANAKIN	Has e'er there been a voyager who hath
	Made journey unto each and ev'ry one? 115
QUI-GON	Nay, nay.
ANAKIN	—In that I shall be primary,
	Should Fate weave me a way from this bleak place.

           [Qui-Gon takes a small sample of Anakin's
                       blood as he finishes the bandage.

QUI-GON	See? Thou art whole again. Now, off to bed.
ANAKIN	What are your good intentions for my blood?
QUI-GON	Naught but to see thou hast infections none. 120
	And now, I prithee, take thy needed rest:
	Tomorrow is a vital day for thee.
	[*Into communicator:*] I bid thee, Obi-Wan, art
	thou about?

Enter OBI-WAN KENOBI, *on balcony.*

OBI-WAN	Aye, Master. How may I fulfill your needs?
QUI-GON	Make thou what keen analysis thou canst 125
	Of this blood sample I send thee e'en now.
OBI-WAN	It shall completed be upon the instant.
QUI-GON	The count of midi-chlorians I need.
OBI-WAN	What strange monstrosity is this I see?
	What cunning twist of nature's pure design? 130
	I ne'er encounter'd such as this before—
	A count of midi-chlorians so vast,
	Surpassing twenty thousand—O, 'tis dire!
	'Tis past all reckoning, past thought or sense,
	What creature can it be that Fate hath wrought 135

To be so strong and powerful as this?
Is it the boy? What wonder to bethink—
His count is higher e'en than Yoda's is.

QUI-GON   No Jedi hath a count so high as that.

OBI-WAN   O, Master, tell me then: what doth it mean?   140

QUI-GON   I do not know. So many things today
Have been beyond my understanding that
I know not what the sum of them shall be.

[Exeunt Qui-Gon and Obi-Wan
from balcony.

Enter DARTH MAUL.

MAUL   Here on the planet Tatooine I've come
To seek the Jedi and the errant queen.   145
The glory of her capture and their deaths
Is expectation sweet unto my soul.

[Darth Maul sends out probes
to search for the Jedi.

Go forth, discerning probes, and seek them out—
Of my sure victory I have no doubt.

[Exit.

SCENE 6.

The podracing grounds at Mos Espa on the planet Tatooine.

Enter QUI-GON JINN, JAR JAR BINKS, *and* WATTO.

WATTO   I would your spaceship see the moment this
Fast race hath been competed. Understand?

QUI-GON	Pray, patience, bluish friend. Thy winnings shall
	Be thine before the double sun hath set,
	And we shall be far gone from this grim place. 5
WATTO	Unless your ship doth then belong to me.
	I warn you, ply no trickstery on me.
QUI-GON	Thou thinkest Anakin shall not prevail?
WATTO	Mistake me not: the boy is talented
	And in him I've a wealth of conference. 10
	The boy, indeed, is credit to your race.
JAR JAR	[*aside:*] 'Tis e'er a double-sided compliment.
WATTO	And yet, methinks, Sebulba shall be first.
QUI-GON	O wherefore dost thou think it shall be so?
WATTO	'Tis but the odds: Sebulba ever wins. 15
	In expedition of his victory
	I've wager'd all my riches. He'll not fail.
QUI-GON	Thy wager shall be mine, if thou dost wish
	To wager more with assets than with words.
WATTO	Eh?
QUI-GON	—I shall wager my new racing pod 20
	Against the boy and his kind mother, too.
	If thou dost win, thou hast the podracer,
	If I do win, their lives are in my hand.
WATTO	Ha ha, you jest! No pod hath equal worth
	As two hardworking, loyal human slaves. 25
QUI-GON	Thou hast it right. Thus wager but the boy.
WATTO	We shall let that old weaver, Fate, decide.
	A chance cube doth reside within my pouch.
	If blue appears, your sky is clear: the boy.
	But if red shows, the other goes: his mother. 30

[*Watto throws the chance cube.*

> *Qui-Gon uses the Force to*
> *make it land on blue.*

You have prevail'd in this, outlander, aye,
But shall not win the race. Thus, little doth
This wager make a whit of diffidence.

Enter ANAKIN SKYWALKER, PADMÉ, SHMI SKYWALKER,
R2-D2, C-3PO, *and* KITSTER.

O, fie! [*To Anakin:*] Bonapa keesa pateeso.
Buki chanaga o wanna meetee   35
Chopodd, eh? Ha ha!
                                          [*Exit Watto.*

ANAKIN   —"Your friend here should cease
His betting lest anon I own him, too."
What meaning's in these enigmatic words?

QUI-GON   I shall tell thee another time. [*To Shmi:*] Good morn!

R2-D2   Beep, meep, beep, squeak, beep, whistle,
                                 whistle, hoo!   40

C-3PO   Space travel soundeth perilous, indeed.

R2-D2   Meep, meep, beep, nee, ahh, squeak.

C-3PO   —I tell thee true,
They never shall convince me to embark
Upon a starship, nay! Were droids suppos'd
To fly, the maker surely would have giv'n   45
Us wings to do so. Nay, no flier I!

KITSTER   O Anakin, 'tis wondrous thou shalt race.
I've ev'ry confidence in thy success
And certain am thou shalt do it this time.

PADMÉ   I pray, what feat shall Anakin perform?   50

KITSTER   To finish th'race.

PADMÉ   [*to Anakin:*] —Thou ne'er hast won a race?
ANAKIN   'Tis possible I ne'er have done so. Nay.
PADMÉ   Yet finish'd e'en the course?
ANAKIN   —Good Kitster hath
           Foreseen aright, my lady: this shall be
           The day I see the end of the podrace.   55
PADMÉ   Aye, so fear I.
QUI-GON   —Thou wilt have swift success.
           Now go ye and prepare, the race begins!
                       [*Exeunt Anakin, Padmé, Jar Jar, Shmi,*
                           R2-D2, C-3PO, and Kitster.
           O Force, in battle steel this soldier's heart.
           Give unto Anakin the strength he doth
           Require to make a goodly run today.   60
           Our hopes all rest upon this worthy lad,
           Who in a time but short hath made his mark
           Upon our story—yea, upon our souls.
           Whate'er befalls, our fate is now with his
           One and the same, fast tether'd life to life.   65
           Thus rise, O Force, and be his constant stay:
           When he doth ride, make his reflexes swift,
           When he meets obstacles, guide then his hand,
           When he doth need quick thinking, be his mind,
           When he is challeng'd, swell his bravery,   70
           And in the end, grant him—and us—success.
           If the Republic would have justice done,
           This boy shall be the linchpin of that cause:
           If he doth win today, we fix the ship,
           The ship then being fix'd, we fly from here,
           We fly and make our way to Coruscant,   75
           In Coruscant we tell the crimes of trade,

The crimes then told, the Federation falls,
The Federation down, 'tis justice done.
It doth begin today with this contest:
This crucial podrace shall prove bust or best.   80

[Exit.

SCENE 1.

The podracing track at Mos Espa on the planet Tatooine.

Enter ANAKIN SKYWALKER.

ANAKIN   How all occasions do inform toward me
            To spur my action here! The Jedi comes—
            Of all the junk shops in all towns in all
            Of Tatooine, he walketh into mine.
            Yea, enters he unto my simple life   5
            Upon the instant my machine's complete.
            My podracer is ready for the nonce
            As though 'twere Fortune's hand that crafted it.
            Now lies their fate—and mayhap mine as well—
            Upon the skill with which I race today.   10
            Be with me, brave gone souls of slaves who pass'd
            Before me, those who work'd and sweated for
            Another's gain. Ancestors mine, be here—
            O, make me quick in my maneuvering,
            And strong in my resolve and my control,   15
            And brave to face those who would do me wrong.
            I ride with what I am and as I may—
            I ride, and in the end it must suffice.

Enter SEBULBA *and other* PODRACERS *below, preparing to race and
waving to the crowd, with* QUI-GON JINN, SHMI SKYWALKER, JAR JAR
BINKS, R2-D2, C-3PO, *and* KITSTER *coming to help* ANAKIN.
Enter FODE AND BEED, *a two-headed creature, commenting aside.*

BEED   Toong mee cha kulkah du Boonta magi!

Tah oos azalus ooval podraces!   20

FODE   Indeed, the sun doth shine and all is calm

For this year's Boonta Classic. Crowds arrive

From all the far-flung territories of

The Outer Rim. Behold, contestants 'gin

To make their preparation on the grid   25

Where our great race commenceth. See them now,

Familiar in our mouths as household words—

Ben Quadinaros, podracer of Tund,

Gasgano, he who hath from Troiken come,

The two-time champion, e'en he: Boles Roor,   30

The reigning winner, swift Sebulba of

The city Pixelito, and the one

Consider'd favorite to win today.

Shall favor smile upon the favorite?

Next, in the front, by pole position near,   35

It is Mawhonic, he of third-eye sight.

And greetings, too, to Clegg Holdfast and his

Sharp Voltec KT9 Wasp podracer.

Returning to th'arena is Dud Bolt,

With the Vulptereen three-two-seven, it   40

Of marvelous construction and design.

Behold one who hath fervent hopes today:

Ody Mandrell, with droid pit team that hath

Establish'd standards new for skill and speed.

And last, one lately come into the fray,   45

Young Anakin Skywalker, local lad.

The standards in procession are display'd

As all anticipate the starting sign.

[A procession is held, with
C-3PO carrying a canopy.

SHMI   O, Anakin, I bid thee: be thou safe.

ANAKIN   Thy words, sweet mother, are like balm to me.   50
                    Thus hear my dutiful response: I shall
                    In ev'ry turn attempt to keep me safe.

                              [Exit Shmi. Sebulba, aside, breaks a
                                        part of Anakin's podracer.

SEBULBA   Uh-oh . . . ha ha! [*Approaching Anakin:*] Bazda
                                                  wahota, shag.
                    Dob'ella Nok. Yoka to Bantha pood'.

ANAKIN   Cha skrunee da pat, sleemo.

                              [Exit Sebulba.

                                        He doth say   55
                    This race shall see the end of me, but nay,
                    Methinks that I shall see the end of it.

QUI-GON   Art thou preparèd, Anakin?

ANAKIN   —Forsooth!

QUI-GON   Then I shall lift thee e'en as thou lift us.

                              [Qui-Gon lifts Anakin into his podracer.

                    I prithee, do remember these few things: 60
                    Fear not, but concentrate upon the moment,
                    Be mindful of thy feelings, not thy thoughts,
                    And utilize what instincts thou dost have.

ANAKIN   Kind sir, I thank thee and shall these obey.

QUI-GON   The Force be always with thee, brilliant boy.   65

                              [Exeunt Qui-Gon and Jar Jar
                                        as Anakin dons his helmet.

BEED   O grandio lust, amu intoe paren':
                    A Jabba o du Hutt.

FODE   —See Jabba here
                    To start our glorious race.

Enter JABBA OF THE HUTT, *aside.*

JABBA	—Tam ka chee Boon'
	Kee madda hodrudda du wundee na.
	Ka bazza kundee hodrudda, ho ho! 70
BEED	Ya pawa culka doe rundee hazzah!
FODE	With Jabba's speech the race may now commence!
	The power couplings are engag'd, whilst all
	Do flee the grid. The race begins anon!

                                       [Exit Jabba.

Enter QUI-GON JINN, PADMÉ, JAR JAR BINKS,
and SHMI SKYWALKER *above, on balcony, spectating.*

SHMI	Are all his nerves beset with fear and angst? 75
QUI-GON	Methinks he shall do well; be not afeard.
PADMÉ	You Jedi have an undue recklessness.
	The queen shall not—
QUI-GON	—Nay, handmaiden, be still.
	Presume thou not to speak for thy great queen.
	She trusts my judgment, e'en as thou shouldst do. 80
PADMÉ	Thou dost assume too much, with pride too great.
FODE	Podracers all, give fire unto your engines!
JAR JAR	O dissen be messee, me no watch . . .

          [Courtiers play a fanfare, signaling the start of the
                     podrace. The podracers fly off, exiting, except
                         Anakin Skywalker and Ben Quadinaros.

ANAKIN	Alack, so swift begun and swiftly stopp'd!
	The others fly, while I am here assail'd. 85
	My engine runneth down—what foul mischance!
FODE	Ahh, look! Small Skywalker hath stall'd at once.

KITSTER   O, Anakin, be gone—take wing and fly!
ANAKIN   The field flies far beyond me, gone. Fie, fie!
FODE   Ben Quadinaros hath some trouble, too.   90
ANAKIN   The systems now respond. 'Tis not too late!
            Go, vessel swift, and help us reach the goal.
                        [Anakin's podracer flies off; exit Anakin.
FODE   Skywalker hath let fly at last. He goes!
            Wethinks he'll find it difficult indeed
            To match the others' speed and take the lead.   95
QUI-GON   [*to Padmé and Jar Jar:*] I bid thee, mark the race
                                        and bring us news.
                            [Exeunt Padmé and Jar Jar.
            [*To Shmi:*] My lady, do not fear: all shall be well,
            For verily the boy's a pilot skill'd.
            He knoweth well the import of this race
            And I believe he shall not fail our hopes.   100

                    Enter JAR JAR BINKS.

JAR JAR   Sebulba knockee Mawhonic, oo,
            He downee onna grounnee hurtsa.
QUI-GON   And what of Anakin? Hast thou seen him?
JAR JAR   He stilla comin' from behinnee—
            Dey comin' to da canyon soonee.   105
                            [Exit Jar Jar Binks.
QUI-GON   The canyon putteth all of them betwixt
            A formidable rock and a hard place.

                    Enter PADMÉ.

PADMÉ   He pulls ahead with speed superior!

Those farthest back he passeth easily—
Mayhap the lad may still the leaders catch.　　110
They disappear'd unto the dark-fill'd caves,
Some other pod and Anakin withal.
Upon the other side did Anakin
Come forth, yet not the other—maybe he
Some misadventure in the tunnel had.

QUI-GON　　I bid thee thanks for this complete report.　　115

                            [Exit Padmé.

SHMI　　He still doth live: thus far, it is enough.

FODE　　Some Tusken Raiders are position'd on
The canyon dune turn, there to fire upon
The hapless racers.

SHMI　　　　　　—Nay? May they do this?

QUI-GON　　E'en if they may not, seemeth it they will.　　120

               [Ben Quadinaros's podracer bursts into
                       flame and breaks into pieces.

FODE　　The last to start is now the first who's finish'd:
Ben Quadinaros' power coupling fails!
Contenders in the ranks now lack by one.

Enter SEBULBA *and other* PODRACERS *on one side.*
All fly through and quickly exit except ODY MANDRELL,
who stops to make repairs to his podracer.

BEED　　Chubba ni chees!

FODE　　　　　　—Sebulba in the lead!

BEED　　Ody Mandrell coona wa wunda dung'.　　125

FODE　　His droid pit team is slow to make repairs.
And what's this we behold? One droid is pull'd
Into his engine, and his pod's destroy'd.

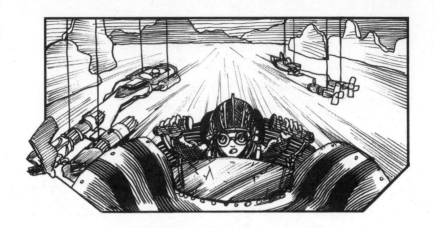

C-3PO	But where is Master Anakin?
R2-D2	—Beep, squeak!
SHMI	Look now, he comes anon. O, Anakin! 130
FODE	Young Skywalker advanceth in the field!

Enter ANAKIN SKYWALKER *and other* PODRACERS *on one side,*
flying through and quickly exiting.

KITSTER	Hurrah!
R2-D2	[*aside:*] —Exciting 'tis, but all's not won:
	Let us not spend our eagerness too soon.
	[*To C-3PO:*] Beep, meep, meep, hoo, squeak,
	whistle, whistle, beep.
C-3PO	Full two more revolutions he must make? 135
	O dear—I fear 'tis two too many, troth.

Enter JAR JAR BINKS.

QUI-GON	What news canst share? Hath he yet passèd more?
JAR JAR	De bad Gasgano stay in frontee.
	No lettee Anakin go passee.

And den Boles Roor did hittee Ani,   140
But he jes' flip and pass him over!

QUI-GON   Your words do testify unto his skill.

                                          [*Exit Jar Jar Binks.*

SHMI   [*aside:*] O, hear my plea, you fates and fortunes all:
Let not my boy meet his untimely end
Upon this field where injury and death   145
So speedily consume whome'er they wish.
He is not made for crushing done in haste,
He'd not be broken by rapidity,
He should not in a hurry meet his end,
He doth deserve a life at his own pace.   150
Instead, let him return for all that shall
Occur in his most strange and charmèd life.
These strangers to his future hold the key,
'Tis plain to me, though 'tis unknown as yet.
Thus, give him all success for their fond hopes.   155
Yet even more, my heart's entreaty is:
Bring him yet safely back into my arms,
That I may tell him of his mother's love.

                          Enter PADMÉ.

PADMÉ   More news: Sebulba plied his trickery
Upon a racer, which did make him crash.   160
The fragments of his podracer ran swift
Past Anakin. Indeed, I thought him gone,
For none could those projectiles large avoid.
Yet I was wrong, the boy did make escape,
And started to draw nearer to the front.   165

QUI-GON   'Tis wonderful.

PADMÉ   —Nay, I have not told all.
              As he approach'd, his cockpit disengag'd
              From one of his two engines. This did throw
              His pod into some disarray. The last
              That I did see, ere hither I return'd,   170
              He had not set his errant pod aright.
FODE   Skywalker spinneth wildly, sans control!
QUI-GON   Go quickly, handmaiden, see what befalls!

                                 [Exit Padmé.

              The lad is clever, madam, and shall make
              This problem into opportunity.   175
              Pray, mark my words: his instincts shall not fail.

                 Enter JAR JAR BINKS.

JAR JAR   Be nottee fraydee, he's okayee!
              The little Anakin did usee
              A magnet, wowsa powafulla,
              He pullee line back to his selfa,   180
              Den reconnect da ting and fixee!
              Den back he go, into da canyon.
SHMI   Thank ev'ry mercy that my son is safe.
              Full many thanks, sweet Jar Jar, for this news.
QUI-GON   Now thither go again to see what's next!   185
JAR JAR   *[aside:]* Mayhap he should go see it for himself.
              Am I his scratching post and eyesight both?
              But soft now, Jar Jar, all is for the good:
              This boy indeed shall fashion our next steps.

                                   [Exit Jar Jar.

FODE   Alas, I care not where thou hailest from,   190
              Such crash shall put thee in a wretched state.

SHMI	What's this of "crash"? What doth the creature mean?
QUI-GON	Indeed, I do not know. Belike our true
	And loyal messengers shall tell us all.
SHMI	It is the knowing not that maketh me 195
	So ache with fear and anguish for my boy.

Enter PADMÉ.

QUI-GON	What now, what news? We heard some tell of crash.
PADMÉ	'Twas not our Anakin. The Tuskens have
	Once more struck from the heights, and with
	their guns
	Did shoot down yet another luckless pod. 200
	By all that's marvelous, the lad still flies,
	And ever nearer to Sebulba draws.

Enter JAR JAR BINKS.

JAR JAR	Behold, iss Anakin. Owooee!

Enter SEBULBA, ANAKIN SKYWALKER, *and other* PODRACERS
on one side, flying through and quickly exiting.

FODE	Against all expectation, as the lap—
	Yea, e'en the final lap—commenceth, 'tis 205
	Sebulba in the front with Skywalker
	Near to his heels, and biting at his lead!
KITSTER	O fly, swift Anakin, and make me proud!
PADMÉ	Pray, do not say the word, Qui-Gon: we go
	To eagerly behold the final act. 210

[Exeunt Padmé and Jar Jar Binks.

QUI-GON	I said so ere this, winsome lady, and
	Declare once more: I sense the boy shall win,
	And when he doth prevail we shall behold
	The swift fulfillment of our mighty hope.
SHMI	Your solace is most reassuring, sir, 215
	Yet I maintain: the mother's sole concern
	Is for the son, and not the broader cause.
FODE	Young Skywalker is forc'd to ride upon
	The service ramp—unfortunate this turn!
SHMI	First down, then up, and next in danger great. 220
	This racing of the pods is made for souls
	Much braver, more courageous than myself.

Enter PADMÉ.

QUI-GON	How now? Art back so soon?
PADMÉ	—'Tis pain t'observe!
	With what abusive knocks Sebulba drives
	The boy aside, e'en to the limit of 225
	The path. 'Twas nearly more than I could bear.
	As Anakin was forcèd far off course,
	It seem'd Sebulba had the lead secure,
	And nothing could disrupt his triumph sure.
	Yet even then all was not lost, in truth— 230
	Another startling turn had Fate to make:
	Like some astounding phoenix rising from
	The ashes where it recently did burn,
	The boy comes swooping o'er the enemy
	And in a blaze of fire doth fly ahead. 235
SHMI	What can this mean?
PADMÉ	—Hear, madam, and believe:

                    The boy hath ta'en the lead.
SHMI   —Ahh, can it be?
                    I almost am more shaken by this news
                    That he could win, than when I did believe
                    He had but little chance.
FODE   —'Tis Skywalker!   240
                    A swift control thrust putteth him on track—
                    Such flying we've not seen for ages. Zounds!

                         Enter JAR JAR BINKS.

JAR JAR   His podracer is breakee breakee!
QUI-GON   What's this? [*To Padmé:*] I prithee, go and see again.
                                                          [*Exit Padmé.*
FODE   Now 'tis some trouble for small Skywalker—   245
                    Sebulba hath again reclaim'd the front.
JAR JAR   De bad Sebulba come behindee,
                    He sneakee up, and Ani scaredee.
                    Den did a part fall off his shippee,
                    Dere lotsa smoke, Sebulba coughin',   250
                    But den Sebulba zoom in frontee.
                    O! Meesa canna take it nowa.
QUI-GON   Divulge yourself, most honor'd, noble Force!
                    Be seen by ev'ry soul that gathers here
                    To watch the pods fly o'er this desert course.   255
                    Show them the power that the Force doth give,
                    E'en to a lowly youth as Anakin.
                    Display the wisdom and experience
                    That one is heir to in the Force's sway.
                    Reveal how weak are those who nothing know   260

Of your astonishing and awesome strength.
Make known here in the sight of this large crowd,
That none succeed who do not know your name.

Enter PADMÉ.

PADMÉ   Another turn upon another turn!
FODE   The lad again doth chase Sebulba's tail—   265
              And nearly hath he overtaken him!
BEED   O inkabunga!
FODE   —Mad the human small
              Most certain be, to make such desperate
              Maneuvers.
BEED   —Punda tah punda.
FODE   —E'en now
              The two are side by side.
BEED   —Bangu du bang'!   270
PADMÉ   The double-man speaks true! Our Anakin
              Had lost his engine—nearly did he wreck—
              Yet manag'd he to bring it back online.
              As they tore through the canyon, Anakin
              Gave chase until he ran not far behind.   275
              Then, with a valor well beyond his years,
              Drew he aside Sebulba, and did hook
              The Dug's fleet pod so that they rode as one.
              At last, when Anakin had all arrang'd,
              He drove his vessel forward, which did blow   280
              Sebulba's pod into a thousand parts.
              A'whining and a'crying in the sand,
              Sebulba is defeated! I expect
              The swift return of Ani's pod anon!

QUI-GON   O, thank the Force!
SHMI   —Past expectation, this!   285

> *Enter* ANAKIN SKYWALKER,
> *crossing the finish line in triumph.*

KITSTER   Hurrah!
R2-D2   —Beep, meep, beep, squeak!
C-3PO   —O merry day!
Mine eyes had not believ'd it possible.

>   *[Exeunt Qui-Gon, Shmi, Padmé,*
>   *and Jar Jar from balcony.*

FODE   How all in joy and frenzied mirth do greet
            This unexpected, wondrous champion!
            The cheer that rises from the thousands here   290
            Is more than we have heard in all our days!

>   *Enter* QUI-GON JINN, SHMI SKYWALKER, PADMÉ,
>   *and* JAR JAR BINKS *to welcome* ANAKIN.

JAR JAR   Yay, Anakin! De clever boyee!
ANAKIN   O mother! Didst thou see? I have prevail'd!
QUI-GON   What marvelous accomplishment, bright star
            Of Tatooine. Thou makest me most proud.   295
            The Force was present with thee here, forsooth.
PADMÉ   [*embracing Anakin:*] We owe to thee our boundless
                                                gratitude—
            When we look'd for a hero, thou didst come.
ANAKIN   Fine lady, if I did but make you glad,
            Then ev'ry nervous turn was worth its pain.   300
QUI-GON   Now, pardon, I must seek old Watto out,
            And claim from him our wages justly earn'd.

>   *[Exeunt Qui-Gon Jinn, Padmé, Jar Jar Binks,*
>   *Fode and Beed, R2-D2, C-3PO, Kitster,*
>   *podracers, and crowd.*

ANAKIN   Thou hadst no need of worry, mother mine:
            Thy boy is safe, is here, and he is thine.
>   *[Shmi takes Anakin in her arms, singing.*
SHMI   [*sings:*] Shall I make merry? O, shall I make mirth?   305
            Thee did I love, since th'instant of thy birth,
            To see thee win is unto my heart gain,

Yet still I fear, and sense some future pain.
Hark! Cracks a mother's heart.
Shall I make merry, O, shall I make mirth?   310
Today thou hast prov'd thy most ample worth,
Thou showest scores of strength to ev'ryone,
And by the showing, shall I lose a son?
Hark! Cracks a mother's heart.
Shall I make merry, O, shall I make mirth?   315
Of quiet moments have our lives a dearth,
The visitors who come are noble men,
Yet when they go, shall I know peace again?
Hark! Cracks a mother's heart.

                                                     [Exeunt.

SCENE 2.

On the planet Tatooine.

Enter QUI-GON JINN *and* WATTO.

WATTO   You vile dissembler, cheat and villain rank—
Somehow I have been swindl'd in your deal.
You knew—by magic most unnational—
The boy would find the will to win the race.
My fortune hath been most unfortunate,   5
And all that I did think to win I've lost.

QUI-GON   And yet the sport is gambling call'd for there
Is e'er the chance that one shall sorely lose.
When one doth walk e'er near th'inferno's edge,
One must expect to burn from time to time.   10
Now to our business: bring thou the parts

Unto the hangar where I'll make my claim.
Thereafter I shall visit thy small shop,
That thou may to my care release the boy.

WATTO   Nay, I shall never let you take him hence;   15
A wager's mollified when one doth cheat.

QUI-GON   Mayhap thou wouldst prefer to talk it o'er
Within the court and justice of the Hutts?
I have no doubt they would take merriment
In proffering a settlement twixt us.   20
I would delight to witness Jabba's face
As thou explainest thine absurd complaint.

WATTO   [aside:] This mention of the Hutts destroys my case.
[To Qui-Gon:] Forsooth, the boy is yours—both
                              be accurs'd!
                                   [Exit Watto.

                   Enter OBI-WAN KENOBI.

QUI-GON   We have the needed parts to take our flight,   25
And may this abject settlement depart.
Yet first must I go thither to complete
A vital matter—I shall not be long.

OBI-WAN   Say, wherefore do I sense that we shall add
Another wretched life-form to our group?   30

QUI-GON   It is the boy who hath made possible
Our flight beyond this planet desolate.
Now our responsibility's to him—
Our path becometh his path, Obi-Wan.
Install the hyperdrive with all good haste,   35
That we may fly the moment I return.
                       [Qui-Gon walks aside.

                           Obi-Wan begins to exit.

OBI-WAN   [*aside:*] What news is this that comes from
                              Master Qui-Gon?
               The four who left our ship shall now be five?
               We have acquir'd a hyperdrive and in
               The acquisition comes a boy as well.   40
               What strange part shops have they on Tatooine
               That do include a lad with ev'ry sale!
               'Tis double-dealing ta'en to an extreme.
                            [Exit Obi-Wan.

QUI-GON   Pray, madam and young Anakin, come forth!

        Enter ANAKIN SKYWALKER *and* SHMI SKYWALKER.

ANAKIN   What is it, sir?
QUI-GON   —First must I render to   45
               Thee what is due: the money for thy pod.
                    [Qui-Gon gives the money to Anakin,
                           who gives it to Shmi.
ANAKIN   Behold, sweet mother—wealth we ne'er have known.
SHMI   'Tis wonderful beyond expectancy.
QUI-GON   Yet I shall render e'en a greater prize:
               Thy freedom thou obtain'd in the podrace.   50
               I say again, young Anakin: th'art free.
ANAKIN   Mine ears do play me tricks: what did you say?
QUI-GON   No longer art thou slave to anyone.
ANAKIN   Hast heard, dear mother? Freedom now is mine!
SHMI   There's naught shall hold thee back now,
                            cherish'd child.   55
               Thou art a free man, free at last to dream
               And make thy dreams into reality.

It is a privilege thou shouldst embrace.
[*To Qui-Gon:*] With all my heart I beg you: take
                              him hence,
Deliver him from this cruel life we lead   60
And make him yet a Jedi like yourself.

QUI-GON   Thy wish is mine as well, and I believe
'Twas no coincidence we three did meet.
The Force knows not of accident nor chance,
But wisely guides our footfalls, one by one.   65

ANAKIN   Then I shall fly within your starship, sir?

QUI-GON   I bid thee, understand now, Anakin:
To be a Jedi's not an easy path,
The training is a task that few endure,
A challenge to the mind and heart and soul.   70
E'en if thou dost in training find success,
'Tis but the prelude to a life most rare
And rife with difficulty sans compare.

ANAKIN   Yet 'tis a life I wish for, have wish'd for.
My mind is settl'd: I shall go with you.   75
[*To Shmi:*] O, mother mine, dost give me leave to go?

SHMI   My son, 'tis not my place to give or take.
This path is set before thee—thou alone.
The choice, therefore, lies not with me, but thee.
Dost thou choose to depart—what is thy will?   80
Know this: no choice that thou canst make herein
Shall alter my unending love for thee.

ANAKIN   Then I shall go—it is mine earnest wish.

QUI-GON   Go then, and swift thy preparations make.

ANAKIN   Hurrah! [*Aside:*] Yet wait, what's this that comes
                                to me?   85
A thought o'er which I'd not reflected yet.
[*To Qui-Gon:*] What of my mother? May she also

come?

QUI-GON   There is no use in hiding truth from thee:
            I did attempt to free her, Anakin—
            I tried as well I could. Yet Watto did   90
            Refuse to let your mother come withal.

ANAKIN   And yet, thou shalt come with us, Mother, yea?

SHMI   My place is here, my future here as well.
            The time hath come for thou to just let go—
            This change shall do thee well, be not afeard.   95

ANAKIN   Why do we worship at the shrine of change?
            Hath change e'er put a meal upon our board?
            Is change a thing to be devoutly wish'd?
            Doth change betoken something positive?
            Or may it be that change for changing's sake   100
            But changes good to evil, bad to worse?

SHMI   Yet change cannot be stopp'd, lest thou would stop
            The sun from setting, or stop death itself.

ANAKIN   How shall a heart be whole that's rent in twain?
            Would that I could be two instead of one   105
            Both boy who doth remain with mother true,
            And man who shall become a Jedi Knight.
            I cannot be a man by staying here,
            Therefore I'll be a boy who takes his leave.

SHMI   Go with my love, my heart, my joy, my life.   110
                    [Anakin walks aside, to his chamber,
                        where C-3PO sits, turned off.
            [To Qui-Gon:] I thank you, e'en though it is difficult.

QUI-GON   I shall look after him: thou hast my word.
            Wilt thou be well?

SHMI   —As well as I can be.

QUI-GON   Thou knowest, I do hope, how much I wish

We could take thee withal. Some part of me   115
Remaineth here, with thee, on Tatooine.

SHMI   Indeed, I know. In taking my sweet boy,
You take with you my heart, and it is yours.
Pray, treat it well.

QUI-GON   —'Twill be my life's pursuit.
And now farewell, dear lady. Be at peace.   120

                              [Anakin turns on C-3PO.

C-3PO   Awake again—good Master Anakin!
I stand a'ready at your service, sir.

ANAKIN   C-3PO, I have been freed today,
And presently must take my leave from thee.
I shall by starship fly from Tatooine.   125

C-3PO   I wish you well, my maker, master, both—
Yet I would wish to be complete ere you
Depart for stars and systems still unknown.

ANAKIN   I beg thy pardon, Threepio, for I
Have not the time to finish thee or give   130
Thee all the coverings thou dost deserve.
I'll miss the time I spent constructing thee,
And e'en though thou art droid, thou wert a friend.
I shall entreat my mother not to sell thee.

C-3PO   Alack, to sell me?

ANAKIN   —Now, adieu.

C-3PO   —O, my!   135

                    [Exit C-3PO. Anakin returns to
                              Shmi and embraces her.

ANAKIN   I cannot part from thee, my mother, nay.

SHMI   O, Anakin, have courage and endure.

ANAKIN   O, think'st thou we shall ever meet again?

SHMI   What is the whisper of thy heart, dear one?

ANAKIN	I do not know; I hope so. I say: aye.	140
SHMI	If thou dost say it, truly it shall be.	
	Keep me within thy heart until that time.	
ANAKIN	I shall return and grant your freedom, too.	
	This is my promise and my solemn vow.	
SHMI	Now go, my son, and look not backward. Yea,	145
	I bid thee, keep thine eyes e'er forward turn'd.	
	O, look not backward.	

                                       [Exit Anakin.

                         Agony most rare!
With ev'ry yearning of this mother's will
I would both let him go and keep him here.
The two desires make duel in me still: 150
The selfish one would keep him for mine own,
The better one would see him go, be free.
That better part hath power o'er my tongue,
Whilst cries the selfish part within my soul.
For one, this is a mother's proudest time,   155
For th'other, 'tis the height of pain and grief.
Such gain, such loss, such blessing and such burthen,
Beyond all measure anguish, joy, and fear.
Was ever mother fortunate as I?
Was ever mother desolate as I?   160
O, Fate, go with these two who leave me now:
The man and boy—nay, rather 'tis two men.
One young, one older, aye, yet both are men.
This is my solace: I did raise the boy,
Did give him all I could whilst he was mine,   165
And now, as a young man, the bird shall fly.
Thus shall my tears turn to a healing balm,
And sighs of sorrow turn to breath of life.

Goodbye, mine Anakin, mine only son:
My life is whole since thine hath just begun.   170
                                        [Exit.

SCENE 3.

On the planet Tatooine.

Enter DARTH MAUL.

MAUL   The Jedi's whereabouts my droids have found,
              And I shall make my strike on them anon.
              I see them now—the older Jedi comes
              With boy of little consequence behind.
              I'll make my swift attack upon the elder,   5
              And finish with the youth once he is dead.

Enter QUI-GON JINN *and* ANAKIN SKYWALKER.

QUI-GON   Behold, what's this? An enemy? [*To Anakin:*] Make
                                                        haste!
              Unto the ship make thou the swiftest flight,
              And tell them to depart most urgently!
                        [*Exit Anakin. Qui-Gon and Darth Maul
                                        begin to duel.*
MAUL   Your pow'rs are weak, and agèd your technique.   10
              You art no match for one so skill'd as I.
QUI-GON   Alas, such speed and fleet agility
              I ne'er have seen but in the Jedi ranks.

Enter Obi-Wan Kenobi, Anakin Skywalker, R2-D2,
Captain Panaka, *and* Ric Olié *on balcony,*
in the cockpit of the Naboo cruiser.

PANAKA	Great trouble doth pursue Qui-Gon below!
OBI-WAN	I prithee, pilot, take off now!
RIC	—I shall!

15

OBI-WAN	Draw near to them—fly low that he may leap.

      [Qui-Gon begins to lose strength.

MAUL	You grow still weaker; soon I'll see you fall.
QUI-GON	Perchance I've one last leap to save myself.

      [Qui-Gon jumps into the ship, on the balcony.

MAUL	This battle ends, and you are barely sav'd:
	Next time you shall not be so fortunate.

20

      [Exit Darth Maul.

ANAKIN	Good sir, is't well with you?
OBI-WAN	—What was the thing?
QUI-GON	I am not certain, merely do I know
	That it was trainèd well in Jedi arts.
	Belike it hither came to take our queen—
	And, lo, the game it plays is dangerous.

25

ANAKIN	What shall we do?
QUI-GON	—For now we bide our time,
	And strive for calm and patience in all things.
	Young Anakin Skywalker, I present
	My strong apprentice, Obi-Wan Kenobi.
ANAKIN	Well met, dear sir. Are you a Jedi, too?

30

OBI-WAN	Indeed, my lad, as well thou mayest be.
QUI-GON	Together we shall this new threat confront—
	Belike we'll answers find on Coruscant.

      [Exeunt.

SCENE 4.

On the planet Naboo.

Enter NUTE GUNRAY, SIO BIBBLE, OOM-9,
and other GUARD DROIDS.

NUTE	Your queen is lost, your people feebly starve,
	And it appears their governor—e'en you—
	May not outlive them. Truth, your life is mine,
	A prize that I do mean to claim anon.
SIO	Your ill-advis'd attack shall gain you nil. 5
	Naboo is proudly a democracy:
	Its citizens decide, and they did speak
	Decisively enough against your rule.
NUTE	Your insolence offends. [*To guards:*] Take him away!

[*Exeunt several guards with Sio Bibble.*

OOM-9   My troops have ta'en position in the swamps,   10
          Where they seek out the underwater towns
          About which rumor hath been spread of late.
          What hidden is shall soon revealèd be.
NUTE   I thank thee, Captain: thy words ease my mind.
          Make me a full report of what they find.   15

                                        [*Exeunt.*

SCENE 5.

Aboard the Naboo cruiser and on the planet Coruscant.

Enter RUMOR.

RUMOR   Whilst cruelly doth the Federation find
          Excuse to starve Naboo's poor, conquer'd hordes,
          Fear starts to rise within each troubl'd mind—
          Look ye, and see how Rumor knots her cords.
          Young Anakin by guilt is overrun,   5
          Thinks he of her he left with sad regret.
          Old Qui-Gon and the younger Obi-Wan
          Consider this portentous recent threat.
          O, how fleet Rumor does her labor—see?—
          Runs to and fro to make them sick with fear.   10
          Unsung is my impact on history,
          Such times as these are wherefore I am here.
          Catch all, I shall, within the net I threw
          And witness each sharp pain they undergo.
          Now, watch as one more cometh into view: 15
          The maiden Padmé, full of care and woe.

                                        [*Exit Rumor.*

Enter PADMÉ.

PADMÉ   By dark of night I come to hear what news
            I can of my defenseless countrymen.
            Would that I could be present with them there
            To share in their torment and suffering   20
            And be handmaiden to their ev'ry hope.
            Yet since, for now, I am a traveler
            And spinning through the echelons of space,
            My path lies not with that of my dear ones.
            Thus must I steal a hidden glimpse of them.   25

                PADMÉ *turns on the computer.*
                Enter SIO BIBBLE *in beam.*

SIO   The death toll hath been catastrophic here.
            Conform unto their wishes, Highness, please,
            And contact me anon, ere more are dead.
                              [Exit Sio Bibble from beam.

                Enter ANAKIN SKYWALKER.

PADMÉ   Sweet boy, how dost thou fare?
ANAKIN   —I'm very ill.
            And how do you?
PADMÉ   —Ahh, very ill, too, lad.   30
ANAKIN   I find the depths of space turn my blood cold,
            The blood that knows the heat of Tatooine.
                              *[Padmé wraps a blanket
                                  around Anakin.*
PADMÉ   Forsooth, thou comest from a planet warm,

Belike too warm for mine own temp'rate taste.
In truth, space is a cold and empty place.   35

ANAKIN   And you: why doth my lady say she's ill?
Your visage could recite a thousand woes.

PADMÉ   The queen is worried; her concern is mine.
The people of Naboo face pain and death.
The queen must make the Senate understand   40
That they must rise anon and intervene
To stop the cruel invasion, else all's lost.
The outcome is beyond what I can see.

                [Anakin removes a pendant from his pouch.

ANAKIN   I fashion'd this small trinket for you, miss,
That you might oft remember Anakin.   45
'Tis carvèd from a snippet of japor—
Perchance it shall bring fortune to your path.

PADMÉ   'Tis passing beautiful, kind Anakin.
Yet need I not a trinket to recall
The brave and solemn boy before me here.   50
Ne'er shall your memory be far from me,
Whether I am adorn'd with this or no.
Pray understand that many things must change
When safely we arrive at Coruscant;
What shall not change is how I care for thee.   55

ANAKIN   My heart doth hold you in its care as well,
Though even this reeks of duplicity,
For how can one heart hold the care for two?

PADMÉ   Thou dost yearn for thy mother kind, I know.
'Tis meet and right to do so, Anakin.   60

                                      [Exit Padmé.

ANAKIN   Then wherefore doth it make my spirit burn?

Enter RIC OLIÉ.

RIC   Attend, lad, we soon land on Coruscant!
             Behold its lights and iridescent glow—
             The planet whole is but one city vast,
             Which giveth light at all times, day or night.   65
             Below, 'tis Chancellor Valorum's craft,
             And there, upon the landing dock, doth wait
             Sir Palpatine, an honorable man.

Enter QUI-GON JINN, OBI-WAN KENOBI, SABÉ *dressed as*
Queen Amidala, PADMÉ, JAR JAR BINKS, CAPTAIN PANAKA, *and,*
separately, CHANCELLOR VALORUM *and* SENATOR PALPATINE.

QUI-GON   With humble mien, we greet ye heartily.
                         [Qui-Gon Jinn and Obi-Wan Kenobi
                                   bow to Chancellor Valorum
                                   and Senator Palpatine.
PALPATINE   And you as well, ye noble Jedi Knights.   70
             [To Sabé:] Your Majesty, 'tis gift to see you well.
             I fear'd the worst, but you are here: alive.
             The dire communications breakdown did
             Upset us quite, and have us all concern'd.
             I shall with eagerness hear your report   75
             Of all that hath befallen since Naboo.
             Straight may I introduce unto your grace
             The Chancellor Supreme, Valorum, he.
VALORUM   Your Highness, I do bid you hearty welcome:
             It is a privilege to meet your person.   80
SABÉ   All thanks, respected Chancellor Supreme.
VALORUM   Your situation is full well distressing,

	The Senate is most strain'd by all the rumors.	
	I've call'd a special meeting of the Senate,	
	Wherein we may your circumstance consider.	85
SABÉ	Most grateful am I for thy deep concern.	
PALPATINE	A question of procedure did arise,	
	Yet I am confident we'll overcome.	
QUI-GON	[*aside, to Valorum:*] Good Chancellor, I must anon	

address

	The Jedi Council. All is not as 'twas,	90
	The situation hath new obstacles.	

[Exeunt Qui-Gon Jinn, Obi-Wan Kenobi,
and Chancellor Valorum as the others move
to Senator Palpatine's quarters.

PALPATINE	My queen, here is there no civility.	
	Aye, no civility: mere politics.	
	What once the strong Republic was it is	
	No longer: weak and feeble 'tis become.	95
	The Senate's rife with babbling delegates,	
	E'er greedy for their taste of power's meat.	
	The common good's become a most rare dish,	
	Unsav'ry to their growing appetites.	
	I would not lie to you, Your Majesty,	100
	There is but little chance the Senate shall	
	Move to suppress or censor this attack.	
SABÉ	The chancellor, it seems, would disagree.	
	He spoke of hope it may yet be put right.	
PALPATINE	And yet, the chancellor hath little pow'r.	105
	He e'er by accusations is beset,	
	All whispering corruption's damning name.	
	Full baseless, yea, but still he lacketh might—	
	'Tis bureaucrats who rule the Senate now.	

SABÉ   I prithee, say: what options have we, then?   110
PALPATINE   'Twould grant us greatest chance of Fate's esteem
            If we could push t'elect a chancellor
            Who could be stronger, verily supreme.
            Belike a one as this could then control
            The bureaucrats and rule for justice's sake.   115
            If you put forth a vote: no confidence
            In Chancellor Valorum, 'twould suffice.
SABÉ   Are you beyond all reason? He hath been
            An ardent friend and patron of Naboo.
PALPATINE   'Tis not the only course: we could, as well,   120
            Submit a plea unto the courts of law.
SABÉ   Which would but take far longer even than
            The Senate in its plodding, snail-like pace.
            Our people groan and die, O, Senator:
            The Federation must be quickly stopp'd.   125
PALPATINE   If we bethink but realistically,
            Your Majesty, it well may be our lot
            To bear the Federation's cruel control—
            Not for eternity, but for a time.
SABÉ   Not even for a second, Senator.   130
            I never shall accept their unjust rule.
            Were we to let it be, e'en for a trice,
            Their vicious claws would sink far deeper in,
            And ev'ry day that pass'd would render their
            Control o'er our most happy, peaceful globe   135
            More palatable for th'Republic to
            Take in: a moment would become a time,
            A time would quickly turn into an age,
            And all would soon forget that e'er Naboo
            Had once been rul'd by its own government.   140

Seek not to make me hide their vice from view,
For this is something that I cannot do.

                                        [Exeunt.

SCENE 1.

On the planet Coruscant.

Enter YODA, MACE WINDU, QUI-GON JINN, OBI-WAN KENOBI,
KI-ADI-MUNDI, *and other members of the* JEDI COUNCIL.

QUI-GON Whate'er it was that fought with me that day,
     'Twas trainèd well in all the Jedi arts.
     'Tis my conclusion, painful though it be,
     That I did face a Sith on Tatooine.

KI-ADI Impossible. The evil Sith have been   5
     Extinct well nigh a thousand years. 'Tis true?

MACE   It seemeth quite unlikely they could rise
     Again, without the Jedi Council's knowledge.
     Indeed, it is unthinkable to me.

YODA   Yet be we mindful   10
     'Tis hard to see, the dark side,
     Hard enough, forsooth.

MACE   Our ev'ry resource we'll to this employ,
     So this dark menace to society
     May swiftly be discover'd. By my troth,   15
     I'll warrant we shall find th'assailant soon.
     The Force be ever with thee, Qui-Gon Jinn.
       [Obi-Wan turns to leave, but Qui-Gon hesitates.

YODA   Good Master Qui-Gon,
     More to say have you to us?
     I bid you, speak it.   20

QUI-GON With your permission, Master, I report:
     A vergence I've encounter'd in the Force.

YODA   A vergence, say you?

Divergent is your news, which
Converges on us.   25

MACE   Located 'round a person? 'Tis a fluke.

QUI-GON   Nay, 'tis a boy: a boy whose cells have stores
Of midi-chlorians that do surpass
The number found in any life-form I
Did e'er encounter, or think possible.   30
Yea, 'tis a number higher than I did
Imagine could be found in anyone.
Perchance the boy was actu'lly conceiv'd
By midi-chlorians, strange though it seems.

MACE   You reference the prophecy that speaks   35
Of one who shall bring balance to the Force.
And you believe it is this fresh young boy?

QUI-GON   'Tis not my will nor place to here presume—

YODA   But presume you do.
Reveal'd your opinion is.   40
'Tis plain enough, hmm?

QUI-GON   I do but wish the boy to tested be.

YODA   Ahh, train'd as Jedi?
For him this is your request?
So certain are you?   45

QUI-GON   It was the Force's will that we would meet.
'Twas not by chance we came unto his shop,
But we were thither brought to set him free,
That he, in turn, would bravely rescue us,
And we together should make journey here.   50

MACE   Bring him before us then, unto our sphere,
And we shall test him in the Council here.

                              [Qui-Gon bows as all exeunt.

SCENE 2.

On the planet Coruscant.

Enter ANAKIN SKYWALKER, *a* GUARD, *and* RABE,
a handmaiden to the queen.

GUARD   The boy doth seek to visit Padmé here.

ANAKIN   Indeed, if 'tis permissible to do.

                                  [Exit guard.

RABE   Apologies, but Padmé is not here.

Enter QUEEN AMIDALA.

AMIDALA   Who is't who comes?

RABE   —'Tis Anakin, who would

Hold one or two brief words with Padmé, Highness.   5

AMIDALA   Upon an errand Padmé hath been sent.

ANAKIN   I take my leave now, to the temple bound,

Therein my Jedi training to begin.

Methinks I never may see her again,

And did but wish to say a fond farewell.   10

AMIDALA   Thy message shall we soon relay to her,

And hear thou this: by royal wisdom we

Are certain that her heart doth follow thee.

ANAKIN   With gratitude I thank Your Majesty.

                       [Exeunt Anakin and Rabe.

AMIDALA   My hope lies past all expectation now: 15

Unto the Senate I am bound at last,

To plead my case and ask for mercy there.

Yet 'mongst the politicians shall I find

A kindly voice to answer mine appeal?

The senator—e'en Palpatine—doth thirst   20
To set things right for us, yet hath consum'd
More than a measure of ambition's drink.
Another friend we've none within the hall
Where the Galactic Senate soon shall meet.
Thus, if the time hath not supplied a friend,   25
I'll fashion one or two with mine own plea.
Mayhap when they behold the regal tears,
Their hearts shall open, blocking out their greed.
I cannot be a man and threaten them,
So shall I with a woman's cunning win.   30
Pray, hold me fast, O Fate, let me not slip:
Support me by your ever-weaving hands.

Enter MEMBERS OF THE GALACTIC SENATE, *including*
SENATOR PALPATINE, CHANCELLOR VALORUM, LOTT DOD *of the*
Trade Federation, and the SENATOR OF MALASTARE.

VALORUM   The high, exalted, and unquestionable
             Galactic Senate now is call'd to order—
             Let harmony be present as we gather.   35
             The chair doth recognize the senior statesman
             Who cometh from Naboo, the sov'reign system.
PALPATINE   Wise Chancellor Supreme, and delegates
             Of this strong Senate, I must make report:
             A tragedy of vast proportions hath   40
             Occurr'd upon our innocent Naboo.
             Its genesis was in this chamber here,
             Taxation of the trade routes its first cause.
             The tragedy engulf'd our planet in
             Th'oppression of the Federation cruel.   45

LOTT	These accusations are outrageous words!
	Unto these statements I object with zeal.
VALORUM	The chair hath not yet seen fit to acknowledge
	The senator from the Trade Federation.
PALPATINE	To speak for our great planet and present 50
	Our allegations solemn and severe,
	I introduce the newly minted queen—
	She of the late election in Naboo—
	Queen Amidala, who shall prick your ears,
	And, if they can be movèd, hearts as well. 55
AMIDALA	O, honorable representatives
	Of this republic we do call our home:
	I speak before you as a broken queen,
	Within your presence due to dire events
	That have of late befallen on Naboo. 60
	Our system hath been senselessly attack'd
	By the droid armies of the Federation.
LOTT	I heartily object! Where is her proof?
	Her words are but an idle tale, spun out
	From some outlandish dream or whim. Instead, 65
	We recommend a quick commission, sent
	To ascertain the truth about Naboo.
SENATOR	The senator of Malastare concurs
	With what the Federation's delegate
	Doth in this matter recommend and wish. 70
	A commission must be sent unto Naboo.
VALORUM	The point is made. Pray, grant me consultation . . .
	[Chancellor Valorum leans aside to
	speak with his advisors.
PALPATINE	*[aside:]* The perfect part the chancellor now plays,
	That I may write the passage I desire.

              [*To Amidala:*] Behold, Your Majesty, the bureaucrats   75
              A group of thespians who craftily
              Do rule the scene upon their stage of pow'r.
              Their coffers by the Federation fill'd,
              They act to bend the chancellor's own thoughts
              And sap his strength by softly spoken lines,   80
              Until the curtain falls and they have won.

VALORUM   The Federation's point hath been conceded.
              Will you, Your Majesty, defer your motion
              That we may soon appoint a keen commission,
              Which shall investigate your accusations?   85

AMIDALA   Nay, I shall not defer nor be deterr'd,
              Nor shall I grant you any deference.
              I come before you here in urgency,
              Not that we may be turn'd aside again
              But that you may resolve this vile attack   90
              Upon our sovereignty even now—
              E'en here, e'en on the very instant. Fie!
              No more of this delay shall I endure!
              My land did not elect me that I might
              Deliver it to suffering and death,   95
              Whilst ye in words both weak and impotent
              Discuss the dire invasion in committee!
              I tell you truly: if incapable
              This body is of acting for the right,
              Methinks new leadership is warranted.   100

PALPATINE   [*aside:*] The trap is set, and she hath sprung it quite.

AMIDALA   I move a somber vote: no confidence
              In Chancellor Valorum's leadership.
                [*The other senators begin chanting their approval.*

PALPATINE   Well done, Your Majesty. They shall elect

Another chancellor—a strong one, sure,   105
Who shall not let our tragedy endure.

[*Exeunt.*

SCENE 3.
On the planet Coruscant.

Enter QUI-GON JINN *and* OBI-WAN KENOBI *on balcony.*

OBI-WAN   Methinks the boy shall never pass the test
            The Jedi Council will before him place.
            He is too old, e'en at his tender age.
QUI-GON   Nay, Anakin shall be a Jedi yet.
            I promise thee, in time it will be so.   5
OBI-WAN   Do not defy the council yet again.
QUI-GON   If I defy them, marry 'tis but what
            The situation calleth for. No more.
OBI-WAN   The council, Master, is within your reach:
            If you but follow'd faithfully the code,   10
            You would be on the council, I suspect.
            Aye, in this matter their thoughts are not yours,
            And they shall not approve of what you wish.
QUI-GON   Thou still hast much to learn, apprentice mine.

[*Exeunt.*

Enter, below, YODA, MACE WINDU, KI-ADI-MUNDI,
MEMBERS OF THE JEDI COUNCIL, *and* ANAKIN SKYWALKER.

YODA   Anakin, young one,   15
            Let thy mind be free, and sense
            What thou dost see not.

ANAKIN   I sense a ship . . . a cup . . . a ship . . . a speeder.

MACE   [*to Yoda:*] The boy hath spoken right in this big

                                                     game.

YODA   Well 'tis, my young one.   20
           Now, speakest thou verily:
           How, pray, dost thou feel?

ANAKIN   In troth, I have been cold since Tatooine.

YODA   Indeed thou mayest,
           For climes as thine much heat give.   25
           Yet afeard art thou?

ANAKIN   Nay, sir, I suffer neither fear nor dread.

YODA   See through thee we can.
           To be brave excellent is;
           Forthright is better.   30

MACE   Be mindful of th'emotions of the spirit.

KI-ADI   Thy thoughts upon thy mother sadly dwell.

ANAKIN   My soul doth hunger for her warm embrace.

YODA   Mmm, a dish of which
           Thou art scared to lose the taste: 35
           A mother's regard.

ANAKIN   Of what import is that unto this test?
           Doth sadness o'er my mother mount to aught?

YODA   Aye, ev'rything 'tis.
           To the dark side of the Force,   40
           Fear's the surest path.

           Fear leads to anger,
           Onward leads anger to hate,
           Hate to suffering.

           A bounty of fear   45
           Is present in thy spirit—

Fear beyond measure.

Enter QUI-GON JINN *and* OBI-WAN KENOBI.

QUI-GON	Wise masters, we have come to hear your will,
	To say what shall become of this brave youth.
KI-ADI	The Force is strong with him; we all do see't. 50
QUI-GON	He shall be trainèd, then? That is your word?
MACE	Nay, though the Force may be unbreakable
	Within the boy, he shall not trainèd be.
QUI-GON	Yet wherefore is this so? What reason is't?
MACE	It is but basic: he hath grown too old. 55
QUI-GON	He is the chosen one. Had ye but one
	Eye working 'mongst you all, it would be seen.
YODA	Mmm, easy 'tis not,
	For cloudy this boy's future
	Appeareth in sight. 60
QUI-GON	Then I shall train the lad, if you will not.
	As Padawan I claim young Anakin.
	The boy hereafter mine apprentice is.
YODA	Your apprentice is?
	Forgotten have you, e'en now, 65
	You've one already?
	'Tis impossible,
	Aye 'tis never permitted,
	That one doth two train.
MACE	Rules of engagement do forbid such plans. 70
QUI-GON	Keen Obi-Wan is utterly prepar'd.
OBI-WAN	Forsooth, I stand a'ready, trials to face.
YODA	Our own counsel shall
	We heed on who is ready.

	Presume not to tell.	75
QUI-GON	The man is obstinate and still hath much	
	To learn about the Force that liveth, yet	
	More capable in skill and strength there's none.	
	Like mother bird who sees her fledgling fly,	
	There's little more I can teach Obi-Wan.	80
	I prithee, let him take to wing and soar;	
	Allow room for a new egg in the nest.	
YODA	Young Skywalker's fate	
	Shall not yet be unravel'd:	
	'Tis work for later.	85
MACE	The present is no time for chirping talk:	
	The Senate shall soon in their chamber vote	
	For their new Chancellor Supreme. This may	
	Cause some unrest within Republic ranks,	
	Put pressure new upon the Federation,	90
	Thus meeting evil with a broader threat.	
KI-ADI	The queen's attacker you encounter'd there	
	On Tatooine may be drawn out by this.	
MACE	It is for you to safeguard this good queen	
	And find out the identity of this	95
	Dark foe beyond a reasonable doubt.	
	We think this shall be circumstance enough	
	To bring to light this myst'ry of the Sith.	
YODA	O, hesitate not!	
	Success we wish you—adieu,	100
	The Force be with you.	

[Exeunt.

SCENE 4.

On the planet Coruscant.

Enter JAR JAR BINKS.

JAR JAR   The course of justice never did run smooth.
Those who are weak by laws are weaker made,
Those who have pow'r by laws are given more.
'Tis near impossible to e'er persuade
The ones with power to surrender it.   5
Indeed, they often claim they've power none,
And cannot see their unjust privilege.
When some gross fault of theirs is then expos'd,
They throw their hands unto the sky and cry,
"O, now 'tis us who sorely are oppress'd!"   10
Thus do the dominating twist the tale
And make themselves the subject of their pity,
Whilst turning blind eye to those truly plagued
By burthens those in pow'r can never know.
'Tis certain that the Senate's powerless   15
And we no justice in its court shall find.
The queen by fear and worry is beset
And cannot make inform'd decisions thus.
We must away, returning to Naboo.
Our hope lies not within the Senate's care,   20
For only double crossing there we'll find.
Our only hope doth lie in joining strengths:
The Naboo and the Gungans fix'd as one,
Leave Coruscant and take the battle home.
The queen shall never listen to a fool,   25
Yet she may be convinc'd by foolish words

If they are spoken by coincidence.
Then shall the notion flourish in her mind
As though it were her own. But soft, she comes!

Enter QUEEN AMIDALA.

	Are yousa thinkin' people gon' die?	30
AMIDALA	I do not know; unclear the future is.	
JAR JAR	And Gungans gettin' pasted too, eh?	
AMIDALA	It is my fervent hope that shall not be.	
JAR JAR	De Gungans no die sans a fightee.	
	We allsa warriors—grand armee!	35
	Methinks that's whysa you no like us.	

Enter CAPTAIN PANAKA *and* SENATOR PALPATINE.

PANAKA	Your Highness, I bring tidings of delight!	
	Our noble Palpatine is nominee	
	To soon succeed Valorum's feeble rule	
	As Chancellor Supreme. Is not this grand?	40
PALPATINE	Surprising 'tis, Your Highness. Welcome, too—	
	If I elected am, I'll put an end	
	To all the Senate's vile, corrupted ways.	
AMIDALA	Who else a nomination did receive?	
PANAKA	One Bail Antilles of old Alderaan,	45
	And Ainlee Teem of Malastare as well.	
PALPATINE	I feel most confident full many votes	
	Of sympathy our cause shall garner us.	
	Forsooth, I shall be chancellor anon.	
AMIDALA	Once you have o'er the bureaucrats control,	50
	I fear our people shall no longer be:	
	Our way of life shall, by then, be destroy'd.	

PALPATINE I understand your worry, Majesty.
     The Federation, though, doth revel in
     Possession o'er our planet even now. 55
AMIDALA Good Senator, this is your chosen sphere—
     Among the politicians you excel,
     Troth, I have ev'ry hope of your success
     And faith in your most shrewd abilities.
     My sphere doth call most urgently to me, 60
     Its voice doth cry with desperation loud,
     And so unto Naboo I must return:
     Where I am needed, thither I shall go.
JAR JAR   [*aside:*] The queen doth walk upon the fool-made
                   path.
PALPATINE Return, Your Majesty? I bid you, pause, 65
     Consider the reality you face.
     If you go back, you shall be forc'd to sign
     The wretched treaty most assuredly.
AMIDALA Nay, hear me now: no treaty shall I sign.
     Whatever Fate hath woven for Naboo 70
     Shall be my final destiny as well.
     Good Captain?
PANAKA   —Highness?
AMIDALA   —Go, prepare the ship.
PALPATINE I prithee, Highness, stay here where 'tis safe.
AMIDALA I have a good eye, Senator; I can
     Yet see a Jedi temple by daylight. 75
     'Tis plain to me that our Republic doth
     No longer function for the good of all.
     'Tis plain that your proud Senate doth exist
     To serve itself, not its constituents.
     'Tis plain that if I would for justice seek, 80
     I must look elsewhere than on Coruscant.

If you would serve me here, bring reason once
Again unto the Senate. Now, adieu.

        [Exeunt Queen Amidala, Jar Jar Binks,
                and Captain Panaka.

PALPATINE   A royal wish doth move my soul no wise,
For I am made to answer no one's wish   85
Save for mine own. This sniv'ling, sullen girl
Shall be but slight impediment unto
The plan for the Republic I'll devise.
Devising shall become division when
I sow the seeds of discord in this place,   90
Which shall spread o'er the galaxy anon.
O, Queen, your words do reek of schoolgirl's moans,
E'er braying for some smear she hath endur'd.
Your actions are no wiser, as you seek
Nobility in death upon Naboo.   95
Yet, 'tis no matter: I shall write the end
I carefully have plann'd despite—or e'en
In spite of—her departure to her home.
My plans shall by no regal deed be still'd,
For I'll perform whatever I have will'd.   100

                       [Exit.

SCENE 5.

On the planet Coruscant.

Enter JEDI 1 *and* JEDI 2.

JEDI 1   Well met, my friend! Say, art thou well?
JEDI 2   —Indeed,

	As merry as the day is long. And thou?	
JEDI 1	A pleasant afternoon I just have spent	
	A'poring o'er the Jedi archives here.	
JEDI 2	What is within to perk thine interest?	5
	I do confess I find them rather dry.	
JEDI 1	O, say not so! The archives are a key	
	That opens up a world of scholarship.	
JEDI 2	I never took thee for a bookish owl.	
	What didst thou find today t'excite thy mind?	10
JEDI 1	A pattern hid within the history	
	Of our vast galaxy leap'd fore my sight.	
JEDI 2	A pattern, aye?	
JEDI 1	—As clear as is the sun.	
	It seemeth each millennium or two	
	There is a backward movement in the Force—	15
	Indeed, in all of life—such that the things	
	That now seem commonplace would, in some years,	
	Seem wildly futuristic.	
JEDI 2	—An example?	
JEDI 1	We have technology appropriate	
	Unto our era, and we Jedi have	20
	Th'ability to leap across large chasms.	
	Imagine, then, if in some future time	
	All life betook a giant backward step:	
	Our ships would duller seem, we Jedi would	
	Not soar and spring as we are wont to do.	25
	Canst thou imagine such a sharp decline?	
JEDI 2	Such retrograde must be impossible.	
JEDI 1	Nay, 'twas the pattern I so clearly saw!	
	More fascinating is: it seemeth we	
	Are due for just another swift step back	30

Within mere decades hence.

JEDI 2   —But can this be?

JEDI 1   The hist'ry doth not lie. If I have done
          The calculations right, within a span
          Of thirty years, we'll see a sharp turn back
          In our technology and Jedi skills—   35
          E'en fashion shall regression undergo.

JEDI 2   What wilt thou do with this discovery?

JEDI 1   I first did think to share with Yoda.

JEDI 2   —Aye,
          'Tis sensible enough as he is wise
          And pure, and serveth on the council with   40
          A voice most fair and just. Keen choice, my friend.

JEDI 1   Yet in the end, 'twas not he I did choose.

JEDI 2   Then whom?

JEDI 1   —The senator, e'en Palpatine—
          A noble sort of fellow, good and kind.
          I shall inform him of the things to come.   45

JEDI 2   Art thou most sure thou shouldst not give this news
          To one among the Jedi, worthy friend?
          If it shall be the Jedi are less skill'd,
          Should not this news be shar'd among our own?

JEDI 1   Alas, we Jedi are becoming known   50
          For our mistrust of others! Troth, this news
          Shall show us ready for collaboration:
          The Jedi and the politicians join'd
          As one in mind, with peaceful harmony.

JEDI 2   Mayhap thou art correct. And even so,   55
          Perchance the pattern thou observ'st is false.

JEDI 1   Would it were so. I would not like to see't!

JEDI 2   I sooner dead would be. Now shall we keep

	Our habit and go dine at Dex's place?
JEDI 1	A pattern I shall haply follow, friend.

60

[Exeunt Jedi 1 and Jedi 2.

Enter QUI-GON JINN *and* OBI-WAN KENOBI.

OBI-WAN	Of disrespect I've none, sir, 'tis but truth.
QUI-GON	The truth, yet from thy certain point of view.
OBI-WAN	The boy is dangerous, they all sense it—
	Say wherefore, then, can you not see it, too?
QUI-GON	What Fate prepares for him is still unclear.

65

In troth, he is no danger, Obi-Wan.
The council shall his future settle, not
Both thou and I contending o'er what's true.
I prithee, let these words suffice for thee
And board the waiting ship; we soon fly hence.

70

[Exit Obi-Wan.

Have I been blinded by ambition's light?
If it is so, it is a grievous fault,
And grievously I may yet answer it.
Yet this small child hath captur'd all my thoughts
As I have not for ages been consum'd.

75

I feel a presence in him that doth stir
My blood and sounds the call of destiny
To meet, befriend, and train this noble lad.
I trust the Jedi Council, yet they did
Not see his exploits in the podracing.

80

Their judgment is distorted by his age;
They see his fear, yet not his aptitude.
I am a Jedi, bound by discipline,
Yet in this matter I shall press the bounds

To bring their hesitation to assent.   85
In doing so, I earn a double share:
The boy is train'd in all the Jedi arts,
The council stretches and in wisdom grows,
And I do reap the benefit of both.
Thus I desire, and trust the Force shall soon   90
Fulfill this noble—if ambitious—work.

　　　Enter ANAKIN SKYWALKER *and* R2-D2.

ANAKIN   I would not be a problem, Qui-Gon, sir.
QUI-GON   I'll warrant thou wilt never problem be.
　　　　　　As yet, I am not given leave to train
　　　　　　Thee, but do ask thee to be mindful and   95
　　　　　　To watch o'er ev'ry move thou seest me make.
　　　　　　Remember, if thou canst: thy focus doth
　　　　　　Determine what shall be reality.
　　　　　　Stay by my side and e'er shalt thou be safe.
ANAKIN   If I may yet another question ask   100
　　　　　　Of midi-chlorians wise Yoda spoke—
　　　　　　Such term is unfamiliar to mine ears,
　　　　　　Pray tell me, what are midi-chlorians?
QUI-GON   Once our vast galaxy did come to be,
　　　　　　Life came to being, wondrous miracle.   105
　　　　　　The energy of all potential life
　　　　　　Was bas'd in these first creatures, which did spread
　　　　　　And soon infusèd ev'ry living thing.
　　　　　　These masters of abundant, pure life force
　　　　　　We now know as the midi-chlorians.   110
　　　　　　The midi-chlorians are life-forms small,
　　　　　　Yea, microscopic are they, and reside

	In ev'ry living being, in the cells.	
ANAKIN	They live within my body?	
QUI-GON	—Aye, inside.	
	All living things are symbionts with them.	115
ANAKIN	From one strange word unto another, sir—	
	I prithee, tell me what are symbionts?	
QUI-GON	Two life-forms that together dwell as one,	
	Each make the other stronger when they're join'd,	
	And both do benefit in the exchange.	120
	These, then, are symbionts. Thus, if there were	
	No midi-chlorians, life would be naught.	
	And neither would we know the Force's pow'r.	
	If we but listen, they e'er speak to us	
	And tell us of the Force and what it wills.	125
	As thou dost learn to quiet thine own mind,	
	Thou shalt, like whisper'd poetry, hear their	
	Majestic voices ringing in thine ears.	
	'Tis like a music written for thy soul,	
	A symphony of words compos'd for thee.	130
ANAKIN	'Tis difficult to comprehend this news.	
QUI-GON	O, thou art not alone, if thou canst not	
	The midi-chlorians yet understand.	
	Yet be thou patient and, in time, thou shalt.	
ANAKIN	[aside:] If I have heard aright, it seems to me	135
	The midi-chlorians make a tough cell.	

Enter QUEEN AMIDALA *and* JAR JAR BINKS.

QUI-GON	Your Majesty, it is our honor to
	Continue in your service and defense.
AMIDALA	Your aid is fully welcome. Palpatine

Believes I do but flee the frying pot 140
To face the Federation's fire at home.

QUI-GON Whilst you are in my charge, I'll chill the threat
Of any Federation flames that rise.
As long as I have breath, I'll guard your life.

JAR JAR Hurrah! Now weesa goin' homee! 145

AMIDALA Methinks it may be trouble we pursue—
If so, we fly to battle on Naboo.

[Exeunt.

SCENE 6.

On the planet Naboo and aboard the Naboo cruiser.

Enter NUTE GUNRAY *and* RUNE HAAKO *on balcony, with*
DARTH SIDIOUS *in beam.*

SIDIOUS Have you the planet verily secur'd?

NUTE We've ta'en control of all the remnants of
The primitives that o'er the planet roam.
Naboo is now in our complete command.

SIDIOUS 'Tis well. I shall, for my part, cause such stalls 5
Within the Senate that all shall remain
Just as it is. The status quo shall hold.
To be assur'd of your continu'd strength,
I shall send my apprentice, e'en Darth Maul,
To help maintain your power o'er Naboo. 10

NUTE Indeed, my lord.

[Exit Darth Sidious from beam.

RUNE —A Sith shall hither come?
Now doth a madness new before us rise.

[Exeunt Nute and Rune from balcony.

Enter OBI-WAN KENOBI, RIC OLIÉ, *and* ANAKIN SKYWALKER
aside, in the cockpit of the Naboo cruiser.

RIC	Those do control the forward stabilizers.
ANAKIN	And these control the pitch?
RIC	—They do, indeed.
	Thou art a student quick and most astute.

15

Enter QUI-GON JINN, QUEEN AMIDALA, JAR JAR BINKS,
and CAPTAIN PANAKA.

PANAKA	Once we do land, the Federation shall
	Arrest your royal person, bind you as
	A common criminal, and force you then
	To sign their awful treaty.
QUI-GON	—I agree.
	I do not see what profit comes of this.

20

AMIDALA	I shall but even out our bottom line,
	And take back what belongs to us by right.
	'Tis not for profit, but for justice's sake.
PANAKA	We few, we happy few, are but too few.
	We have no army that can match their count.

25

QUI-GON	I can protect you, but can fight no war.
AMIDALA	'Tis understood. I call on Jar Jar Binks.
JAR JAR	You wantin' meesa, Youra Highness?
AMIDALA	I do. The queen hath need of thy kind help.
	[Obi-Wan, Ric, and Anakin join the others.
RIC	As we did land, a battleship was seen

30

	Upon our scopes—a single one, 'tis true,
	Yet one shall be enough to give us chase.
OBI-WAN	It was a droid control ship, orbiting.

PANAKA	Belike they saw us as we landing made.
OBI-WAN	To make it brief: time runneth short for us. 35

[Exeunt.

Enter RUMOR.

RUMOR	Below, upon the ground, a hope doth wait,
	E'en as the ship doth land, all have new fears.
	Herein all those on board shall find their fate—
	O, how it frightfully unknown appears.
	Look now, as I do make their hearts afraid, 40
	Determin'd, yet deterr'd by all their doubt.
	The final act shall on Naboo be play'd,
	Hath Rumor set the pieces to work out?
	E'en now, the Jedi start to doubt their place:
	Guards they shall be unto the queen no more. 45
	Uniting these two people face-to-face—
	Naboo's hopes to ensure—is not their chore.
	Good soldiers of the queen become nonpluss'd
	And e'en Queen Amidala, in her breast,
	Now hath, by Rumor's will, more doubt than trust: 50
	Shall they on Jar Jar all their future rest?

Enter QUI-GON JINN *and* OBI-WAN KENOBI.

OBI-WAN	Toward the Gungan city Jar Jar's gone.
QUI-GON	'Tis well.
OBI-WAN	—Think you the queen's idea shall fly?
QUI-GON	The Gungans shall not easily be sway'd;
	Thus let us hope the urgency's enough 55
	To give wing to Her Majesty's idea.

	We cannot use the pow'r we have to help,
	As we are peacekeepers, not warring men.
OBI-WAN	Good Master, what e'er comes, I'd have you know:
	For my behavior I apologize.
	'Tis not my place to disagree with you
	About the boy, and hearty thanks I feel
	That you should think me ready for the trials.
QUI-GON	Thou art a keen apprentice, Obi-Wan,
	And art a wiser man by leagues than I.
	'Tis clear, as I upon the waters of
	Thy future gaze, that thou shalt navigate
	What is to come with grace, be pilot of
	A wondrous course, a winsome Jedi Knight.

60

65

Enter JAR JAR BINKS *(from water),* SABÉ *dressed as Queen Amidala,*
PADMÉ, ANAKIN SKYWALKER, R2-D2, CAPTAIN PANAKA,
RIC OLIÉ, *other* NABOO SOLDIERS, *and, separately,*
MEMBERS OF THE QUEEN'S COURT.

JAR JAR	Nobody's dere! De Gungan city
	Deserted is. Some fight, me thinkin'.
OBI-WAN	Think'st thou they have been taken to the camps,
	Where Federation's foes are all intern'd?
PANAKA	Belike the Gungans all have been destroy'd.
JAR JAR	Yet meesa nowee think so, Captain.
QUI-GON	Dost know where they may be, meek Jar Jar? Eh?
JAR JAR	When trouble come, they go place sacred.
	Come, meesa show you it! Come withee!

70

75

All journey to the Gungan sacred site. Enter BOSS NASS,
other GUNGAN BOSSES, *and* CAPTAIN TARPALS.

TARPALS	Your honor, wise Boss Nass, I do present
	Queen Amidala, ruler of Naboo. 80
JAR JAR	Hello, de big Boss Nass, your honor.
NASS	O, Jar Jar Binks, now who's da uss-en uthers?
SABÉ	I am Queen Amidala of Naboo.
	I come before your royal court in peace.
NASS	Naboo biggen. Youse bringin' mackineeks, 85
	And yousa bringin' trouble, all bombad.
SABÉ	We humbly come before you to suggest
	Betwixt our peoples an alliance strong.
PADMÉ	Your honor.
NASS	—Whosa diss? And why she speak?
PADMÉ	I am Queen Amidala. This is but 90
	My decoy, my protection, loyal guard.
	She speaketh for me when it serves the time,
	But you, Boss Nass, deserve the rightful queen.
QUI-GON	[aside:] The handmaiden had play'd a hidden hand,
	And dealt us all an unexpected shock. 95
PADMÉ	For this deception, my apology;
	'Twas necessary to protect myself.
	Your honor, hear my deferential plea:
	Though our two peoples have not e'er agreed,
	Our two societies have liv'd in peace. 100
	The vile Trade Federation hath destroy'd
	All we have work'd so ardently to build.
	If action is not swift, all shall be lost.
	I call on you to help us. [Kneeling:] Nay, I beg—
	A queen's humility giv'n for your aid. 105
	Myself and those with me are servants now.
	[The Naboo, the Jedi, and Anakin Skywalker kneel.
	You work the loom of our yet unknown fate.

NASS	Ha! Yousa nowa thinkin' yousa great
	Beyond de Gungans now. Me lika dis!
	Mayhap shall be dat weesa bein' friends. 110
PANAKA	I shall away, to learn what may be found
	That may be advantageous to our cause.

        [Exit Captain Panaka. The Gungans and the Naboo
               embrace and then begin forming battle lines.

      Enter Nute Gunray, Rune Haako, *and* Darth Maul
      on balcony, with Darth Sidious *in beam.*

NUTE	Our strong patrols have been sent forth, my lord.
	Their starship in the swamplands hath been found.
	It shall not be too long ere they're destroy'd. 115

SIDIOUS   An unexpected play this is for her.
                 'Tis too aggressive. [*To Darth Maul:*] Mindful be,
                                                            Lord Maul.

                 Pray, let them be the first to make a move.
MAUL   Indeed, my master, just as you do say.
SIDIOUS   She is more foolish than I e'er did think.   120
NUTE   All troops have been dispatch'd unto the swamp
                 Where she with her small force assembles now.
                 It doth appear she's join'd with primitives.
SIDIOUS   This shall be an advantage to us, quite.
NUTE   I may proceed, then?
SIDIOUS   —Yea. Destroy them all,   125
                 Erase all trace or memory of them.
                                 [*Exeunt Nute Gunray, Rune Haako,*
                                 Darth Maul, and Darth Sidious from beam.
NASS   [*to Jar Jar:*] O, yousa doin' grand, good Jar Jar. You
                 Hat uss-en and Naboo together brought.
                 Thus, weesa make you bombad general!
JAR JAR   A general! O meeso happy!   130

                 Enter CAPTAIN PANAKA *with several* NABOO SOLDIERS.

QUI-GON   Good Captain, how doth our position stand?
PANAKA   They have ta'en nearly ev'ryone to camps.
                 There are, as yet, some hundreds who have form'd
                 An underground resistance movement here.
                 Full many as I could, I've hither brought.   135
                 So far's the news that we may count as good,
                 Yet there is more that rings a grimmer note:
                 The Federation's army is more vast
                 And far more pow'rful than we first bethought.

	Your Highness, I believe we'll not prevail—	140
	I fear this battle may undo us quite.	
PADMÉ	This battle's but a side dish to the main—	
	A savory diversion to the feast.	
	The truer course shall elsewhere be array'd,	
	A table we shall in the city set.	145
	Keen R2-D2, furnish us the plans.	

[R2-D2 *projects a beam showing a map of the city.*

	The Gungans hither draw the droidly throng,	
	Whilst we make way into the city by	
	The hidden passage near the waterfalls.	
	Once we obtain unto the entrance main,	150
	Panaka shall a new diversion craft.	
	This being done, we others shall go forth	
	Into the palace, capturing the viceroy.	
	Sans him, they shall be lost and sore confus'd,	
	And thus, the day is ours. What do you think?	155
QUI-GON	A cunning plan, if all doth go as hop'd.	
	The viceroy shall be guarded thoroughly.	
PANAKA	It shall take pains the throne room to obtain,	
	But once therein, it shall be easier.	
QUI-GON	There is an ample possibility	160
	That in this action many Gungans fall.	
NASS	Ahh, weesa all prepar'd to do ours part.	
PADMÉ	We have a plan that shall immobilize	
	The army of the droids. Our pilots brave	
	Shall fly unto the droid control ship, which	165
	E'en now doth make its orbit, and destroy	
	It utterly, disabling all the droids.	
QUI-GON	A plan most well-conceiv'd, and dangerous.	
	The risks are bounteous, as well you know.	

       Your fighters' weapons may not penetrate   170
       The large ship's shields.

OBI-WAN   —An even greater risk:
       If it doth happen that the viceroy 'scapes,
       He shall another army bring to bear.

PADMÉ   'Tis clear, then, why we must the viceroy take—
       No different conclusion shall suffice.   175
       Upon that ending all our hopes begin.

R2-D2   Beep, squeak! [*Aside:*] O, cause most noble—
                                 may it rise!

[Exeunt Qui-Gon, Obi-Wan, Padmé, Anakin, Sabé,
Captain Panaka, Ric Olié, R2-D2, and Naboo soldiers.
Gungans begin preparing for battle.

Enter GUNGANS *riding fambaas.*

TARPALS	The shields we now be starting up. Make ready!
JAR JAR	[*aside:*] O, sight that bringeth tears unto mine eyes:
	The Gungans brave astride their fambaas raise 180
	A shield that shall protect us verily.
	This is the moment for which I have liv'd,
	To see my sore oppress'd and careworn folk
	Rise with one voice and hope with the Naboo.
	O shield, give us protection from this war, 185
	O shield, be our defense against the wrong,
	O shield, guard all our peaceful future days,
	O shield, let we beleaguer'd souls have rest.
TARPALS	Behold, there in the distance, foes they come!
JAR JAR	[*aside:*] The battle hath begun, and 'tis our time— 190
	This day shall live fore'er in song and rhyme!

[*Exeunt, marching toward battle.*

SCENE 1.

On the planet Naboo.

Enter QUI-GON JINN, OBI-WAN KENOBI, PADMÉ,
ANAKIN SKYWALKER, R2-D2, CAPTAIN PANAKA,
NABOO SOLDIERS, *and* PILOTS, *including* RIC OLIÉ,
across from BATTLE DROIDS.

QUI-GON   Pray listen, Anakin: once we're inside,
             Thou shouldst be hidden and await us there.

ANAKIN   Indeed, sir. Aye.

QUI-GON   —Await us there—move not!
             [The Naboo forces begin dueling with battle droids.
                     Exeunt Naboo soldiers and battle droids.

PADMÉ   Anon, good friends, let us toward the throne,
             Where we shall take the viceroy by surprise.   5

Enter NUTE GUNRAY, RUNE HAAKO, *and* DARTH MAUL *above,*
on balcony, observing the battle on a screen.

NUTE   Methought the battle would be far from here!
             How is't that they the courtyard have achiev'd?
             This is too close. O, shall this mean our end?
             [Exeunt Nute Gunray, Rune Haako, and Darth Maul.

Enter more BATTLE DROIDS, *engaging in combat.*

OBI-WAN   The battle is upon us now—press on!
             We speedily rush t'ward the hangar to   10
             Release the pilots to the skies above.
             Courageously these men and women fly

To strike the ship that doth control these droids!

QUI-GON Young Anakin, the time is now—flee, hide!
And stay thou in one place till this fight's o'er.   15

ANAKIN I go, kind sir, and shall await you here.

R2-D2 Beep, meep, beep, whistle, squeak, beep, meep,
nee, hoo!
[*Aside:*] Abide with him I shall, and keep him safe.
[Anakin and R2-D2 run aside to take cover.

PADMÉ Ye pilots brave, make for your ships and fly!

QUI-GON They go, amidst the constant blaster fire,   20
They go to serve our hope with their own lives!
Take wing, ye gentles all, and aid our cause!

R2-D2 Beep, whistle, hoo! [*Aside:*] This zealous ship
hath pull'd
Me whole within to ready for a launch.
Alas, the pilot who would lead me falls!   25
What shall I do?

ANAKIN   —The blaster shots fire fast
And quick, just barely passing by my head.
I shall be safer in the cockpit of
This ship that here doth sit without an owner.
[Anakin climbs aboard the ship into
which R2-D2 has just been placed.

OBI-WAN The droids are all defeated: for a time   30
We have some rest. Yet it shall surely pass.

PADMÉ The viceroy must within the throne room be.

PANAKA One group, two groups—red group, blue group—
make haste!
Attend me now, come join our latest quest.

ANAKIN Pray, wait for me, I come anon.

QUI-GON   —Nay, stay!   35
Thou shalt be safe within that armor'd ship.

ANAKIN   But I would follow.
QUI-GON   —Hear my words: remain
              Within that cockpit till we do return.

                    Enter DARTH MAUL.

              [*To Padmé:*] This fight is ours. Your Highness,
                                        fare you well.
PADMÉ   We'll to the throne room by another route.   40
                        [*Exeunt Padmé, Captain Panaka,*
                                and other Naboo soldiers.
QUI-GON   I know not who you are or what you want,
              Yet I do have skills most particular,
              Acquir'd throughout a Jedi's long career.
              These skills do make me nightmarish to such
              As you. Surrender now, and you shall live—   45
              If not, you shall be dead, and there's an end.
MAUL   I'll not be taken by you, man naïve;
              Your feeble skills are naught when match'd to mine.
              This is the moment I have longèd for:
              Two Jedi to assuage mine appetite.   50
OBI-WAN   We are no feast for you, O wretched knave.
QUI-GON   Lay on, you Sith, and by us be you damn'd!
                        [*Exeunt Qui-Gon, Obi-Wan,*
                                and Darth Maul, dueling.

                    Enter DROIDEKAS, *firing.*

ANAKIN   We must do something speedily, R2!
R2-D2   Beep, meep!

ANAKIN	—I know not where the trigger is.
	I'll try this button here—but wait, what's this? 55
	This vessel doth begin to fly—'tis live!
	Ahh, here are the controls that operate
	The guns—feel ye the taste of laser fire!
	[Anakin shoots, destroying the droidekas.
R2-D2	Squeak, whistle, nee!
ANAKIN	—It flies of its own will.
	Hold steady, R2—fly we into space! 60
	[Anakin flies aside.

Enter RIC OLIÉ *and* PILOTS *aside, in space,*
with FEDERATION FIGHTERS *opposing them.*

RIC	Be cautious all, 'tis fighters straight ahead.
BRAVO 2	Forsooth, good Bravo Leader.
BRAVO 3	—Aye, indeed!
R2-D2	Beep, squeak, beep, whistle, meep!

ANAKIN	—Behold, R2,
	Our comrades there do fight the errant foe.
	The autopilot takes us there e'en now. 65
	Although by this machine I am drawn forth,
	It echoes my desire as well, as though
	'Twere I who had programm'd this speedy ship.
	Away to heav'n, respective lenity,
	And fire-ey'd fury be my conduct now. 70
	Let us away, and thither join the fray!
RIC	The shield deflector's much too strong for us!
ANAKIN	This fighting is intense beyond all reason.
	I prithee, R2, do thine expert work
	And from this autopilot give release 75
	Before we both are cruelly kill'd herein!
R2-D2	Beep, whistle!
ANAKIN	—Clever droid, R2—hast done!
	Let us unto the portside deviate.
R2-D2	[aside:] This boy, methinks, hath still a manner wild—
	Mayhap he thinks this is a podrace field. 80
	[To Anakin:] Meep, squeak?
ANAKIN	—Return? Why no, it shall not be.
	The master Qui-Gon order'd me direct
	To stay within the cockpit of this ship.
	I shall fulfill his mandate to the word—
	The letter of the law is thus fulfill'd, 85
	E'en if, in doing so, the spirit's snubb'd.
R2-D2	Meep, woo, beep, whistle, squeak, beep, whistle, nee!
ANAKIN	'Tis plain we are in trouble. Pray, hold fast!
	This battle is my first, may be my last!

                   [Exeunt.

SCENE 2.

On the planet Naboo.

Enter JAR JAR BINKS, CAPTAIN TARPALS, *and other* GUNGANS
fighting BATTLE DROIDS, *stage left.*

JAR JAR   [*aside:*] Thus far the battle is not ours or theirs.
            Their tanks could not pull down our mighty shield,
            Yet now have they made breach with countless droids.
            I ne'er imagin'd such a massive force
            As that the Federation did release.   5
            'Twas hundred, nay 'twas thousands of the droids,
            All lin'd up rank on rank to work us woe.
            'Twas more than we could bear—thus we retreat.
            We flee, but still the fool hath crafty tricks.
            A battle droid lies broken on the ground,   10
            Yet blaster shall not come loose from its grasp.
            Thus, jump upon it now, and trigger fire,
            Destroying other droids that are nearby!
            This fool is not so foul against a foe.
            Clutch tightly, hands, around the catapult,   15
            Releasing all the power'd spheres within.
            Though they are meant to fly into the air,
            They do as well a'rolling on the ground
            And striking our grim enemies mid-spin.
            Now for the final act, the fool's finale   20
            Make use of this small sphere, a boomer, aye,
            And strike this droid and his vast battle tank.
            The droid hath been defeated, but alack—
            We are surrounded by a thousand more.
TARPALS   No gibben up now, General Jar Jar,   25

           For meesa tink of something.

DROID 1   —Hands aloft!

JAR JAR   O, meesa do surrender quickee!

           [Jar Jar Binks, Captain Tarpals, and other Gungans
              freeze as they are surrounded by battle droids.

         Enter PADMÉ, CAPTAIN PANAKA, *and* NABOO SOLDIERS,
            stage center, fighting with BATTLE DROIDS.

PADMÉ   Good Captain, we've but little time for this—
           The droids do not concern us. Only shall
           The viceroy's capture and defeat give us   30

               The victory we sorely need today.

PANAKA   Let us, then, by another path make way.

                       [Captain Panaka shoots the windows.

               Your Highness, go! As 'twere a wingèd bird,

               Our group shall to the throne room make ascent,

               Brave soldiers, let fly your ascension guns!   35

                   [Padmé, Captain Panaka, and Naboo soldiers
                           rise to the balcony with pulleys.

PADMÉ   Make entrance to the throne room, where we shall

               Our enemies with arm of valor meet.

PANAKA   We go with you, my queen—would die with you!

Enter DROIDEKAS *and* BATTLE DROIDS *on balcony, threatening.*

PADMÉ   Your wish may be, O captain valiant.

               They now have won, if temporarily.   40

                   [Padmé, Captain Panaka, and Naboo soldiers
                       are escorted to the throne room.

Enter NUTE GUNRAY *and* RUNE HAAKO.

NUTE   Your tiny insurrection makes its end

               E'en now, Your Highness of conspiracy.

               You shall anon put writing hands to use

               And sign the treaty ere the hour is o'er.

               In doing so, you give us victory   45

               And cease the Senate's meaningless debate.

Enter SABÉ *dressed as Queen Amidala and*
other NABOO SOLDIERS.

SABÉ	Cruel Viceroy, hear the rightful queen's decree:
	Your occupation shall conclude at once!
NUTE	Pursue her, droids! [*Indicating Padmé:*] This one's
	a decoy rank!

O clever ruse—but shall not be for long!   50
[Exeunt Sabé and Naboo soldiers, pursued
by droidekas and battle droids.

PADMÉ	Act swiftly, Captain—we shall win the day!
PANAKA	I prithee, men, block all the exits out.

[The soldiers shut the doors.

PADMÉ	Perhaps you did believe that as I am

A ruler young, I'd not bring you defeat.
Yet in the present moment you'll discern   55
The meaning of my generation's strength.
Not made for weakness or timidity,
My rule is one of wisdom past my years.
The youth whom you did think to overthrow
Is now the queen who ends your treachery.   60
Thus shall we here a treaty new devise,
Wherein you part forever from Naboo.
[Exeunt Padmé, Captain Panaka,
Nute Gunray, Rune Haako, and soldiers.

Enter ANAKIN SKYWALKER and R2-D2, stage right.

R2-D2	Woo, nee!
ANAKIN	—We have been hit, R2, we fall!

[Anakin flies inside the Federation's
droid control ship.

Confus'd within this ship, but not yet slain.
I fain would stop, but cannot seem to do't!   65

At last, collaps'd inside an unkind ship,
Full many battle droids approach me now.
Still, all's not lost, R2 restoreth pow'r.
Pray, put the strong shields up for our defense,
Then perish, droids, with sweet torpedo's kiss!   70
                    [*Anakin fires at the droids, then fires into*
                        the hallway leading to the reactor.

R2-D2   [*aside:*] The boy, by chance, hath hit th'reactor main!
             [*To Anakin:*] Beep, squeak, meep, whistle, whistle,
                                        beep, meep, hoo!

ANAKIN   I see it, R2—let us fly with haste!

            Enter DAULTAY DOFINE *and* TEY HOW, *aside.*

TEY   The ship is losing power, sir! The main
             Reactor fails.

DAULTAY   —Nay, 'tis impossible!   75

            Enter RIC OLIÉ *and other* PILOTS.

BRAVO 2   Behold that blast—it cometh from within!

RIC   'Twas not our shot that did so smite the ship.

BRAVO 1   And still, I'll warrant, we shall not complain.

PILOTS   Hurrah!

ANAKIN   —We fly beyond its walls, R2—
              This truly is what podracing should be!   80

BRAVO 1   Look, sir, 'tis one of ours from the main hold.
                    [*The Federation ship explodes, killing*
                        Daultay Dofine, Tey How, and droids.

RIC   The victory is ours, let us make cheer!

> [*Exeunt Anakin Skywalker, R2-D2, Ric Olié, and*
> *pilots. Amid the Gungans stage left, the droids fail.*

JAR JAR   What ho? Was'n they doin' fallin'?

TARPALS   The droid control ship hath just been destroy'd!

JAR JAR   Ha! They all broke-ed. We be savee!   85
           [*Aside:*] And if they triumph thither, on Naboo,
           Two peoples shall be join'd in union true.
> [*Exeunt Jar Jar Binks, Captain Tarpals,*
> *and Gungans in merriment.*

SCENE 3.

On the planet Naboo.

Enter QUI-GON JINN, OBI-WAN KENOBI,
and DARTH MAUL, *dueling.*

QUI-GON   He parries with such speed as doth amaze—
           I ne'er have seen a Jedi move this quick.
           'Tis like the crash of thunder when it sounds,
           Or like the wind that rushes through the hills.
           When once I think I've caught him, he doth fly   5
           With stamina most awesome to behold.
           I almost would his sprightly moves admire
           Were they not us'd to strike upon my life.

OBI-WAN   A double lightsaber he wields with ease,
           Each end a deadly kiss of viper's tongue.   10
           How like a snake he slithers from our grasp
           And snaps at us with kicks and jabs severe.
           He knocketh Master Qui-Gon down, whilst I
           In vain do seek to gain the upper hand.

Then I am knock'd as well, as Qui-Gon fights.   15
With such proficiency this Sith doth use
The Force to duck and dodge and move things, too.
Shall this be th'end, or shall we yet prevail?

MAUL   Ha, by these two I'll not defeated be.
This old man here and his apprentice weak   20
Are no match for the infamous Darth Maul!
Were it but one against me here 'twould be
Already done—the Jedi would be slain
And I stand tall, triumphant. Yet the two
Present a challenge—hap'ly I do greet it!   25
Come, fools, deliver unto me your lives!

QUI-GON   The power generator cavity
Unknowingly we three have stumbl'd 'pon.
He thumps on Obi-Wan, who falls below
Onto another platform. Feel my blow!   30

MAUL   I fall, yet do not fear the landing, nay—
For falling is but prelude to a climb.
Ere he hath from the dais jump'd to me,
I'm on my feet, for battle well prepar'd.

OBI-WAN   Methinks I did unto this chasm profound   35
Near lose my life. More careful I must be!
Now Qui-Gon is alone to fight the beast,
And I must soon return to give him aid.

MAUL   Into a hall of rays I have been press'd,
Such rays as shall a person slice in twain.   40
The lightsabers with which we fight are naught
Compar'd to fiery blaze of these sharp lights.

                    [A beam appears between
                    Qui-Gon Jinn and Darth Maul.

OBI-WAN   Behold—my master and the wretched Sith
            Are separated by a deadly beam,
            Whilst I am well behind, too far to strike.   45
            The Sith doth pace about, much like a cat,
            Whilst Qui-Gon kneels and with the Force communes.

QUI-GON   [*kneeling:*] Be still, my soul, the Force is on thy side.
            Be silent, heart, and let thy raging cease.
            Be quiet, mind, and to this time assent.   50
            Be calm, my body, take the proffer'd rest.
            I know not whether I may yet prevail,
            Or if this shall become old Qui-Gon's end.
            If I defeat this foe, still doubts remain:
            Who is behind this killer's presence here?   55
            And how did they arise again, the Sith?
            'Twould be a better ending if I could
            Subdue the foe and question him at length.
            Yet murther is within his aspect. Yea,
            He shall not let me live another hour   60
            And shall not answer any query pos'd.
            'Tis he or I shall live—or die—herein.
            Ye Jedi ancestors, hear now my plea:
            If I do slay him, help us find the source
            Of this most strange and frightful newfound threat.   65
            If 'tis my time to die, let it be swift
            And painless, let my spirit fly with grace.
            I think upon the things that I have done,
            And those things yet undone that I would do,
            Mayhap they shall not be, when I am gone.   70
            A tragic and a weighty thought is this.
            Mine only cares are for the wondrous boy,
            And for my young apprentice, Obi-Wan,
            And for the Jedi in whose name I serve.

If now the time for me is come, O ghosts   75
Of Jedi past and gone, I ask but this:
Protect my friends, for they are all my life.

OBI-WAN   I must prepare, the beam shall disappear.

MAUL   You fool, e'en now your ending draweth nigh.

[The beams disappear. Qui-Gon and
Darth Maul begin to duel.

OBI-WAN   My master fights with purpose full renew'd!   80
How quickly he doth press toward the beast.
The beams have gone—be jubilant, my feet!
Make haste to run, aid Qui-Gon in the fight.

[The beam appears again, separating Obi-Wan
from Qui-Gon and Darth Maul.

So near I was, yet not quite near enough.
I train mine eyes and hope upon the two: 85
With both I seek the outcome I desire.

MAUL   He had th'advantage, but the tide has turn'd.
His weakness do I sense as he doth tire.
I push him, stun him, strike the blow forsooth!

[Darth Maul runs Qui-Gon through
with his lightsaber.

QUI-GON   Et tu, Sith? Then fall, Qui-Gon Jinn!

OBI-WAN   —Nay, nay!   90
You beastly villain, feel my anger's wrath!

[The beams disappear. Obi-Wan and
Darth Maul begin to duel.

I strike, and cold revenge doth warm my soul,
So like a flash of lightning I attack.

MAUL   With strength renew'd he fighteth for his friend,
Avenging this old man with sharpest strikes.   95
He hopes to claim the life that I have ta'en,

	But little doth he know I shall take two.	
OBI-WAN	Vile foe—I swipe, and this is the result:	
	Your double lightsaber is singl'd out.	
	'Tis now a fight more even, and shall be	100
	E'en fairer when I take the life you owe,	
	The one that you from Master Qui-Gon stole.	
MAUL	Not so, foul boy. You have the upper hand,	
	But yet have turn'd your back upon the chasm.	
	And now, whilst o'er my lightsaber you fret	105
	I strike with th'Force and send you falling down.	

> *[Darth Maul uses the Force to strike*
> *Obi-Wan and knock him into a chasm,*
> *where Obi-Wan grasps a nozzle.*

OBI-WAN	Alas, I fall! My lightsaber is gone,	
	Yet still I cling and am not finish'd yet.	
	E'en as I hang here, grasping for my life,	
	I know how much doth hang upon this duel.	110
	Be patient, Obi-Wan, be calm in mind.	
	Think carefully about thy movement next,	
	Lest it shall be the final one thou mak'st.	
MAUL	He hangeth there, but just prolongs his death.	
	'Tis either down into the endless pit	115
	Or up above, where, with no lightsaber	
	His death shall be as swift as I allow—	
	Or slow, perhaps, so he shall beg for it.	
OBI-WAN	'Tis certain I cannot go down from here,	
	So must ascend with mighty upward leap.	120
	This much he shall expect, yet shall he think	
	I am unarm'd—which, in the main, is true.	
	However, in my mind's eye I behold	
	Another weapon I may master yet.	

Now to it, Obi-Wan: earn thy revenge!   125
      [Obi-Wan flips upward, using the Force to
      pull Qui-Gon's lightsaber into his hands.
      As he lands, he then cuts Darth Maul
      in two using the lightsaber.
Let vengeance howl! The Jedi so decides.
      [Darth Maul falls into the pit.

QUI-GON   Good Obi-Wan?
OBI-WAN   —What ho! He liveth still.
QUI-GON   It is too late for me, dear Obi-Wan.
Yet one thing doth remain: I pray, attend:
But promise me thou shalt train Anakin.   130
OBI-WAN   Yea, Master, yea.
QUI-GON   —He is the chosen one.
Forsooth, he shall bring balance to the Force.
Train him! My spirit goes; I can no more.
      [Qui-Gon Jinn dies.

OBI-WAN   O noble man, by treachery o'erthrown!
A mightier and better Jedi ne'er   135
Did roam the corners of our galaxy.
The light that hath so shone within my days
Hath here been snuff'd most rancorously out.
Yet let it not be said his death's for naught,
Nor that he fac'd his end with anything   140
That's less than perfect valor, bravery
Beyond the pale of what a man should show.
He went unto his death as unto life:
With energy, with passion, and with strength.
How fortunate I am to be his last   145
Apprentice, aye, to learn so much from such
A brilliant star as he put in the sky.

We did but pale when he shin'd forth—nay, not
When he did shine, but as he still doth shine,
And ever shall, until the universe   150
Itself is dark and all's but memory.
Farewell, my valiant master Qui-Gon Jinn,
Deep peace be yours until we meet again.

                                                            [*Exit.*

SCENE 4.
On the planet Naboo.

Enter OBI-WAN KENOBI, QUEEN AMIDALA, CAPTAIN PANAKA,
ANAKIN SKYWALKER, NUTE GUNRAY, RUNE HAAKO,
and many NABOO SOLDIERS *and* CITIZENS.

AMIDALA   O, Viceroy, get you gone and ne'er return.
             You must unto the Senate go and tell
             How your abuse of power did occur,
             How you attack'd a people innocent,
             How you conspir'd with men of evil deeds,   5
             How you did seek to conquer brave Naboo.
PANAKA   It seems your dream of harsh, unending pow'r
             Hath interrupted been and shall ne'er be.
                          [*Exeunt Nute Gunray and Rune Haako
                          escorted by Captain Panaka and guards.*

Enter YODA, MACE WINDU, KI-ADI-MUNDI, MEMBERS OF
THE JEDI COUNCIL, *and* CHANCELLOR PALPATINE.

PALPATINE   We are indebted to you heartily,
             Courageous Obi-Wan Kenobi. Aye,   10

                    And thou, young Skywalker, with interest
                    We shall watch o'er the progress of thy days.
AMIDALA   Congratulations on your grand election,
                    Good Palpatine, now Chancellor Supreme.
PALPATINE   Your spirit bold hath sav'd our sweet Naboo,   15
                    'Tis you to whom congratulation's due.
                    As one, we two together shall bring peace,
                    Prosperity and joy to the Republic.
                              [Exeunt all but Yoda and
                              Obi-Wan Kenobi, who kneels.

YODA   Confer on thee, now,
                    The level of Jedi Knight   20
                    The Council doth. Rise!

                    Yet agree with this—
                    Taking as Padawan th'boy—
                    I do not, indeed.
OBI-WAN   Yet Qui-Gon had a strong belief in him.   25
YODA   Mayhap 'tis correct
                    That the boy's the chosen one.
                    Belike it is true.

                    Nevertheless, O!
                    A danger grave foresee I   30
                    In his being train'd.
OBI-WAN   Wise Master Yoda, I did give my word
                    To Qui-Gon as he knock'd upon death's door.
                    I will train Anakin, and can, and shall—
                    Without approval of the council, if   35
                    Indeed it doth come to that point and time.
YODA   Qui-Gon's defiance

Is greatly renew'd in thee.
Need that thou dost not.

Agree with thy wish   40
The council doth, despite me.
The boy shall be train'd.

Thy new apprentice
Anakin Skywalker is.
The Force be with thee.   45

[Exit Yoda.

Enter QUEEN AMIDALA, ANAKIN SKYWALKER, JAR JAR BINKS,
CHANCELLOR PALPATINE, R2-D2, BOSS NASS, NABOO CITIZENS,
and GUNGANS *in celebration.*

ANAKIN   What is the path that I shall follow next?
OBI-WAN   The council hath permission granted that
            I may take you as my new Padawan.
            Thou wilt be train'd by me, if it shall suit.
            Thou shalt a Jedi be, I promise thee.   50
ANAKIN   I stand prepar'd to follow and obey.

Enter YODA *and* MACE WINDU,
above on balcony.

MACE   There is no doubt: the man mysterious,
            The one who slew Qui-Gon, he was a Sith.
YODA   Always two there are.
            'Tis no more and no fewer: 55
            Master, apprentice.

MACE   Yet who was he destroyèd in the shaft?
            The master or apprentice? None can say.
NASS   O, strike up, pipers! Sing us merry songs!
                        [*The people of Naboo and the*
                        Gungans join together in song.
CITIZENS   [*sing:*] Fly happily upon your feet,   60
            Sing ho and be ye merry!
            The wretched foe hath seen defeat,
            O, be ye merry! Very!
            Our frightful battle all is done,
            Sing ho and be ye merry!   65
            Naboo and Gungans now are one,
            O, be ye merry! Very!

The strife is o'er, the woe is pass'd,
Sing ho and be ye merry!
And now sweet peace hath come at last,   70
O, be ye merry! Very!

> [Obi-Wan Kenobi, Queen Amidala,
> and Anakin Skywalker come forward
> as all freeze.

ANAKIN The first adventure hath both come and gone,
And in its tranquil outcome we find rest.
Toward the future we now look with hope,
And seek to enter it with spirits brave.   75

AMIDALA A boy took his first step on th'Jedi path,
A Jedi from a killer sav'd a queen,
A queen releas'd her people from a threat,
A people made sweet peace with neighbors kind.

OBI-WAN New friends were made, another dear friend lost, 80
And all hath grown by this experience.
These star wars end in celebration here,
Despite the pain, betrayal, hurt, and fear.

Enter CHORUS *as epilogue.*

CHORUS With beating drums a'pounding in the air
And standards wav'd in flight above each head,   85
With decorations streaming o'er the square
And marching Gungans, joy is here widespread.
Young Anakin, now dress'd as Padawan,
Doth give a knowing nod unto the queen.
His master Jedi Knight, e'en Obi-Wan,   90
Looks on as Jar Jar rides his kaadu keen.
The Jedi Council watches the parade,

And Palpatine's odd visage none can probe.
Boss Nass walks forth in pomp, his help repaid
As Padmé offers him a glist'ning globe.   95
This globe of peace o'er all Naboo holds sway,
Whilst falls the curtain on our merry play.

                               [Exeunt omnes.

END.

AFTERWORD.

Let's begin with the hot-button issue: any retelling of *The Phantom Menace* must address Jar Jar Binks. Jar Jar is perhaps the most hotly debated character in cinematic history—some loathe him, whereas others love him (witness any child under age twelve). In *William Shakespeare's The Phantom of Menace*, I did two things with Jar Jar. First, his speech from the movie is transcribed into iambic pentameter . . . almost. In fact, I reimagined Jar Jar's dialogue from the movie in lines of nine syllables, meaning he is one syllable short of a pentameter (yes, like being one sandwich short of a picnic). The other Gungans all speak in full iambic pentameter while maintaining their accents. The second thing I did was to make Jar Jar keenly aware of what's going on around him. In my version of the story, Jar Jar was exiled not because he nearly destroyed the Gungan city, but because of his radical ideas. Banished to the surface of Naboo, he learned human speech and syntax and sharpened his thoughts about how difference races interact. He recognizes, then, that although Qui-Gon and Obi-Wan may be very useful to him and his people—they are Jedi, after all—they also treat him as a savage. (This recognition is backed up in the movie, with Qui-Gon derisively calling Jar Jar "a local" while speaking to Obi-Wan—right in front of Jar Jar!) In this play, Jar Jar is a radical thinker who—using his simple speech pattern—conforms to the humans' expectations of him in order to bring hope to the Gungans, a long-disrespected race.

Other characters get some fun moments, too. Watto is my Dogberry (from *Much Ado about Nothing*), trying to impress people and misusing words in the process. Podrace commentators Fode and Beed, being a two-headed creature, speak as "we" in the first person, not "I." I even gave them a "wethinks" instead of "methinks," for good measure. Chancellor Valorum speaks only with weak endings (an unstressed eleventh syllable at the end of the line), since his character is nothing but a weak puppet. And each line of Mace Windu has a little something special thrown in for the Samuel L. Jackson fans.

Going back to the podrace: how do you capture ten exciting minutes of high-speed, on-screen action in a stage play? My strategy was to make this like a battle scene in Shakespeare's works, with messengers—in this case Padmé and Jar Jar—running in and out describing what's going on, with all-seeing Fode and Beed adding bits of good and bad news as well. Meanwhile, the racers enter and exit quickly as they complete their laps. I imagined the actors running from one side of the stage to the other as they jockey for first place. In a live stage production, these elements would bring at least some of the urgency and excitement created by the high-speed race in the film.

One of the fun things about writing the *William Shakespeare's Star Wars* series is that I am learning more and more about Shakespeare's language. In Shakespeare's time, generally speaking (though with Shakespeare there are always exceptions), "thou" is used informally, as between friends, and "you" is used more formally. "Thou" is also used to express superiority over someone—if you are my subordinate, I will refer to you as "thou," but you will refer to me as "you" as a sign of respect. In the original *William Shakespeare's Star Wars* trilogy I was looser about "thou" versus "you"—beginning with *William Shakespeare's The Phantom of Menace* the distinction is, hopefully, clearer.

Diving into the prequels has been more fun than I expected. Reimagining the characters introduced to us in *The Phantom Menace* as characters involved in an intricate Shakespearean plot gave me new insight into and interest in the film as a whole. I hope the same is true for you.

ACKNOWLEDGMENTS.

This book is dedicated to my wonderful college friends Heidi Altman, Chris Martin, Naomi Walcott, and Ethan Youngerman. Thank you, all of you, for who you are and who you have been for me.

Thanks to my parents, Beth and Bob Doescher; my brother Erik; his family Em, Aracelli, and Addison; and my aunt Holly Havens.

When I started this project, I got together with a group of key people to discuss the challenges and the opportunities the prequels present. Thank you to my good friend Josh Hicks, fangirls Jessica Mason and Kristy Thompson, the encyclopedic Dan Zehr, and Ethan (again) and Erik (again).

Thank you to the wonderful people of Quirk Books: editors Jason Rekulak and Rick Chillot, boss-man Brett Cohen, publicity mavens Nicole De Jackmo and Suzanne Wallace, the heroic Eric Smith, and everyone else at Quirk. Thank you to my agent, Adriann Ranta, for the patience of a saint. Thank you to Jennifer Heddle at Lucasfilm and illustrator Nicolas Delort, both of you a delight.

Continued special thanks to my college professor and friend Murray Biggs.

Thank you to the usual suspects: Audu Besmer, Emmy Betz and Michael Hoke, Jane Bidwell, Travis Boeh and Sarah Woodburn, Chris Buehler and Marian Hammond, Erin and Nathan Buehler, Jeff and Caryl Creswell, Ken Evers-Hood, Mark Fordice, Chris Frimoth, Alana Garrigues, Brian Heron, Jim and Nancy Hicks, Anne Huebsch, Apricot and David Irving, Doree Jarboe, Alexis Kaushansky, Rebecca Lessem, Bobby Lopez, Andrea Martin, Bruce McDonald, Joan and Grady Miller, Jim Moiso, Janice Morgan, Michael Morrill and Tara Schuster, Dave Nieuwstraten, Julia Rodriguez-O'Donnell, Scott Roehm, Larry Rothe, Steve Weeks, Ryan Wilmot, Ben and Katie Wire, and members of the

501st Legion.

To my spouse, Jennifer, who sacrificed time with her husband to assorted Jedi, Sith, and Gungans: thank you, Love. To our children, Liam and Graham: I love you even if you think the prequels are better.

LOOK FOR

WILLIAM SHAKESPEARE'S STAR WARS PARTS IV, V & VI

SONNET 20,000
"Much Ado about Browsing"

Our little play doth end with a beginning
As Anakin is train'd as Jedi Knight.
Our heroes rest, content from all their winning,
Though still another evil hides from sight.
For now, midst merriment our play doth end,
Yet thou, mayhap, shalt say with voice depress'd:
"May I no more my precious time expend
With this grand book? For lo, I am obsess'd!"
Fear not—online these *Star Wars* do abide:
Thy fervor may boost our **book trailer's** views,
And thou mayst see the **educators' guide**,
Or Ian Doescher's **interview** peruse.
The only menace thou couldst e'er design
Is if thou didst not visit us online!

quirkbooks.com/phantomofmenace